# Quintus

# Quintus

by

## R. WEERSTAND

*A story about the
persecution of Christians
at the time of Emperor Nero*

**INHERITANCE PUBLICATIONS**
**NEERLANDIA, ALBERTA, CANADA**
**PELLA, IOWA, U.S.A.**

**Library and Archives Canada Cataloguing in Publication**
Weerstand, R
    Quintus : a story about the persecution of Christians at the time of
Emperor Nero / by R. Weerstand.

Translation of: Quintus.
ISBN 978-1-894666-70-1
    1. Persecution—Juvenile fiction. 2. Nero, Emperor of Rome,
37-68—Juvenile fiction. I. Title.
PZ7.W4334Qu 2006 j839.3'1362 C2005-907479-5

**Library of Congress Cataloging-in-Publication Data**
Weerstand, R.
    Quintus : a story about the persecution of Christians at the time of
Emperor Nero / by R. Weerstand ; [translated by C. Bonker].
       p. cm.
    ISBN: 978-1-894666-70-1 (pbk.)
    Summary: Witnessing the cruelty of the emperor Nero during the burning
of Rome, sixteen-year-old Quintus, a tent maker, must decide how to
reconcile his own beliefs with those of the new Christian religion.
    1. Christianity—Fiction. 2. Persecution—Fiction. 3. Rome—History—
Nero, 54-68—Juvenile fiction.  4. Rome—History—Nero, 54-68—Fiction.
I. Title.
PZ7.P9366Quin 2006
[Fic]—dc22

                                                            2005035742

Previously published under the same title in Dutch by Jan Haan N.V.
Groningen, The Netherlands

Translated by C. Bonker
Illustrations by Hein Kray
Cover Photo: *The Colosseum in Rome, Italy at Night* by Bryan Weinstein

3rd edition co-published in 2006 with:
Pro Ecclesia Publishers
www.proecclesia.com.au

Published in Canada by Inheritance Publications
Box 154, Neerlandia, Alberta T0G 1R0
Tel. (780) 674 3949
Web site: http://www.telusplanet.net/public/inhpubl/webip/ip.htm
E-Mail  inhpubl@telusplanet.net

Published simultaneously in U.S.A. by Inheritance Publications
Box 366, Pella, Iowa  50219

Printed in Canada

# Contents

# Chapter 1

# *A LIFE AND DEATH STRUGGLE*

Syrius thrust out but Gerdonius skillfully met the attack and the weapon slid off his shield. He immediately counter-attacked and Syrius dodged the deadly sword only in the nick of time. The two men circled each other again. The fear of death could be seen in their eyes, burning feverishly, as they looked for a weak spot in the defense of their adversary. An undefended side or perhaps a moment of carelessness could offer the chance of killing the opponent.

Thus these two men fought their life-and-death struggle; it was either victory or death. No other choice was possible.

Were Syrius and Gerdonius such irreconcilable enemies? On the contrary, they were good friends. But why then that merciless fight? It was obvious that it was not a mock battle. Syrius carried a net in his left hand and in his right hand a long pole topped by a steel trident with frightfully sharp points. He thrust the pole purposefully and with all his strength at Gerdonius' chest. Again Gerdonius met the attack with his shield. Was this the way friends treated each other? Certainly not, but then again they were not fighting by choice. They had been forced into this terrible combat because they were gladiators by profession.

In the past they had been free men and Syrius, the Syrian, and Gerdonius, the German, had belonged to the armies that had dared to fight against the Roman legions; the one in the woods and swamps of the north and the other on the hot plains of Asia Minor. Unfortunately, they had become prisoners of war and were taken to Rome by the triumphant army of Nero. As was the custom in those days, they had been sold as slaves and because of their athletic build and great physical strength, had been placed in the school for gladiators.

It was there that Syrius and Gerdonius — the names given to them — had first met each other. Soon they had become firm friends. Now they were opponents in the arena, with one instruction: that the one should kill the other. If they did not do that, or tried to spare each other by pretending to fight, both would be killed. So they had no choice. The victor would be the one who would survive. And both wanted to stay alive! That is why they could not think of their friendship. Each fought to save his life.

In this way they continued to fight. Gerdonius launched into his opponent and Syrius counter-attacked by attempting to render Gerdonius defenseless by throwing the net over his head.

Thousands of onlookers were watching the spectacle in the arena. They were all free Roman citizens, and it was for their enjoyment that these games were held. Being a nation of soldiers, one could not give the Romans anymore enjoyment than to let them watch a life-and-death struggle in which only deftness, strength, and courage could give a chance of victory.

And therefore, on this morning in March of the year 64, they had come to the amphitheatre to see the contest between Syrius and Gerdonius. There were more than one hundred thousand seats, most which were occupied, because the Syrian and the German were both well-known fighters.

The spectators, especially those in the seats at the rear, stretched their necks in order not to miss anything of the splendid scene. They encouraged the two fighters by shouting loudly. They cheered and clapped their hands when one of the two skillfully repelled an attack or cornered his opponent. Things were coming to a climax. Of the twenty-five groups that had started the combat, Syrius and Gerdonius were the only pair left fighting. The other forty-eight had finished their game. Consequently twenty-four bodies were lying in the arena in pools of blood, surrounded by broken weapons. Twenty-four strong young men had been killed to provide some amusement for the public.

Now everyone's attention was turned to the two remaining men. The tickets used for betting on the outcome of the fight, moved quickly from hand to hand. The stakes were very high. Sometimes the poor, who did not have any money, staked their freedom on it. This added to the excitement of the gamble.

Nero was sitting in the imperial box, with his household and some of his senators. While a faint smile played about his thin, bloodless lips, his eyes wandered around the arena. He looked at the colourful scene of the well-filled amphitheatre: the flapping awnings with red, yellow, and blue stripes, the spectators, the Pretorians — the Emperor's bodyguard — in their splendid uniforms and plumed helmets, and the commoners in their scarlet and purple togas. Occasionally the traditional white toga was still seen, although its use was becoming increasingly rare as it was difficult to keep them clean.

"The people are very amused, Seneca," Nero said, turning to his tutor sitting next to him.

"That's not surprising! The duel of those two barbarians is first class, oh divine Caesar," the senator answered, "although it seems to me that Gerdonius is getting tired."

Seneca was correct. The gladiator's breath was becoming jerky. His bloodshot eyes were making his sight hazy. He tried to correct this by shaking his head vigorously. He must not lose the battle. His life was at stake! Oh, if only he could hang on a little bit longer than Syrius; then he would be safe. Safe, yes, but only till the next fight, which could be in a few days time. Still, he did not give that a thought. Any second could be a gladiator's last. He wondered if his opponent was also weakening.

Gerdonius felt strength ebbing rapidly. Then the net was thrown over him. His arm weighed heavily and could no longer ward it off. Yet he was able to block another stab of the trident with his shield, but the blow made him lose his balance and fall. According to the rules of the game, Gerdonius, although not injured severely, had lost the combat.

The spectators, wild with excitement, cheered Syrius. Yet they had great respect for the way in which the conquered gladiator had fought, and the cry "Thumb up, Caesar!" was heard throughout the stadium.

This meant that Nero was asked to spare Gerdonius' life. It was the custom that the Emperor decided whether the defeated man, if he had not been killed in combat, was allowed to live. He made his decision known by holding out his clenched fist with the thumb out. If the thumb pointed down the victor had to kill his opponent, while pointing the thumb up meant mercy.

Syrius had placed his right foot on Gerdonius' chest and turned toward Nero, awaiting his decision.

"The people are asking for mercy, Caesar," Seneca said.

"Let them ask." The reply sounded indifferent. Nero held out his fist without pointing his thumb up or down. The tension in the amphitheatre rose.

The onlookers cheered and shouted. Some more bets on the outcome of Nero's decision were made quickly.

"Aren't they excited?" said the Emperor, while his fat, round face broke into a cruel grin.

"The people are right in asking for mercy for Gerdonius, oh Caesar. He has fought courageously and doesn't deserve to be killed," the senator pleaded.

"A barbarian deserves nothing," was the cutting answer.

"But, oh divine Caesar, of late you have already ordered many gladiators to be killed. Their number diminishes more quickly than we can replenish them."

Nero frowned.

"So you openly confess that you are unable to maintain the number of gladiators?" he asked menacingly.

The senator paled. Such an accusation could mean his death. And Nero had a reputation for sowing death and ruin all around him. He did not care about anything; not about poor Gerdonius either who was waiting for his decision in

11

torturing uncertainty. Yet, the Emperor first wished to continue the conversation.

Meanwhile Seneca had found a suitable reply. "Oh divine Caesar, you misunderstood me. What I meant was: in your incomprehensible wisdom you have already sent so many gladiators to the gods — so that, after your death, you can watch them fight again — that you might have a shortage of them during your earthly life."

"Very well said, Seneca," Nero answered with a treacherous smile. "And because this barbarian is an excellent gladiator, I want to be sure to see him fight again in the realm of the gods."

While saying this, Nero gesticulated vigorously with his thumb down.

Syrius lifted the trident and with force thrust it into Gerdonius' chest. Briefly the body doubled up. Then it was over.

Syrius stumbled out of the arena. He was worn out because of the combat and he grieved bitterly about the loss of his friend.

The crowd cheered him. They had really enjoyed themselves.

# CHAPTER 2

## *QUINTUS*

While the slaves cleared the battlefield, the public left the arena. Quintus, a tall, sturdy, sixteen year old, was among the thousands of people who shuffled to the exits.

Despite his youth he was already a first class Roman: somewhat proud of his citizenship and treating everyone and everything that was not Roman with haughtiness. And, just as his fellow-countrymen, he placed all his trust in his own strength and abilities. His black hair was cut short and his laughing, brown eyes were set in an open and honest face.

Willingly he let himself be carried with the crowd and, indeed, this was the only thing he could do. The narrow exits were extremely crowded. As he slowly moved forward, Quintus glanced at a notice that hung next to the gate. It announced the fights that had just been held. It did not cross his mind that of the fifty men mentioned on the notice, he had seen twenty-five of them murdered, and that only to satisfy people who had a longing for sensation. The "games" were a normal Roman event. Life simply would not be the same without them. What else could one do with ones leisure time if there were no games? And the gladiators? Well, they were only barbarians, slaves, or criminals! Gladiators were things, not human beings.

Meanwhile Quintus had reached the street: the Via Appia. Although he was outside the theatre now, he could not move any faster than before. Via Appia was Rome's main street. It was only six metres wide and the enormous crowd, which had left the amphitheatre, now filled the entire street. The oncoming traffic, wanting to leave the city, struggled against the stream. The donkey-drivers pushed their way through with the greatest of difficulty. Shouting loudly, they drove the animals on. Now and then their whips hit a passer-by, and it is doubtful whether this always occurred by accident.

A little further on the situation improved somewhat when the road divided in two. To the right, by passing under the two aqueducts, the Aqua Marcia and the Aqua Appia, one could reach the Coelian Hill. The headquarters of the Foreign Legion was situated here.

Quintus, however, took the Via Appia and it did not take him long to reach the point where this road changed into the Via Sacra — The Holy Road. This road was used for triumphal processions and was decorated extensively with sculptures. The victorious legions used it to pass the forum where the Emperor took salute.

When Quintus approached the centre of Rome the traffic chaos increased. As he was born and bred in the city he was used to this bustle. He had never known the narrow streets other than packed with people; people of all nationalities — Greek, Asians, Egyptians, Moors, Germans, and many more. The Jews, who formed a complete colony in Rome, were also there. Everyone spoke loudly in their native tongue, as they fought their way through the heavy traffic.

Suddenly the crowd was pressed together as they tried to make room for a senator who was seated in a palankeen — a covered chair that could be carried. The chair was carried by four big negro slaves. Other slaves went ahead shouting at the top of their voices: "Make room for the noble Artotrogus!" Their words were emphasised by the rods in their hands and they did not hesitate to use them. Quintus only just managed to avoid being hit. He yelled at the slaves, but they were used to this and did not take any notice.

"Who does Artotrogus think he is!" somebody asked.

"Tomorrow he will be dead anyway because Nero has ordered him to open his veins," someone else added.

The palankeen passed by and the congestion diminished. It looked like a ship sailing through the water, cleaving the waves with its bow and closing them immediately behind the stern. Quintus let himself be carried along with the stream of people.

Among the public were numerous merchants who tried to sell their goods. This increased the chaos considerably. Quintus noticed a man who was selling grapes, and tried to reach him because he was thirsty. Yet it was in vain because before he had managed to get to the other side of the street he had passed the grape merchant by at least ten metres.

"Next time better," he grumbled.

A bit further along there was a disturbance. Someone had fainted due to the crush of the crowd and was trampled on. This kind of "traffic accident" was an everyday occurrence in the city of Rome. Although Quintus was only a hundred metres from where it occurred, he did not see anything of the mishap. The victim had been taken away quickly and carried into a house. The beggars took advantage of these of "riots," and sometimes even caused them. The more people that were together, the greater the chance to collect some money. One of them approached Quintus.

"Go away!" he snapped. "Tomorrow there will be distribution of free bread in Trans Tiber."

"But I have to eat today too, don't I?" whined the beggar.

The fellow had a firm grip of his tunic and to get rid of him Quintus handed him a coin out of his purse.

"Jupiter will reward you," the beggar responded.

"I hope he will burn a hole in your hand with his lightning so that you will lose the coin," Quintus said spitefully.

The beggar grinned, already grabbing hold of another victim.

At last Quintus had reached the Porticus Margaritaria, a wide street with bazaars. Here the congestion was less intense than at the Via Sacra. However, the noise at this shopping-centre, the most important in Rome, was bewildering. With loud shouts, the shopkeepers recommended the goods they had displayed on tables.

The greatest noise came from the corner where the sellers of wind-instruments were situated. Most customers wanted to try out an instrument before buying it.

Quintus stopped there briefly, not because he intended to buy a trumpet or another instrument but because he had spotted a street urchin who was loitering around the table displaying the instruments. The merchant was arguing with a customer about the sound of a horn. Both men were standing with their backs to the street. The urchin had approached unseen and suddenly Quintus realised what the boy had in mind. Among the instruments was an exceptionally long trumpet, the mouth-piece of which was facing the street. The bell of the trumpet lay very close to the customer and the shopkeeper.

The boy was ready to play his trick. He glanced at the men to make sure that they had not noticed him. Then he drew his lungs full of air and blew the trumpet as loud as he could. His face became as red as beetroot but the effect exceeded even his most hopeful expectations. The two men jumped in fright when they heard the high pitched noise behind them. The bystanders laughed while the boy bid a hasty retreat.

Laughing, Quintus proceeded on his way. It had not been very clever of that merchant to display the instrument in that position. No lad can resist such an invitation.

Quintus now arrived at a quieter part of the street: a corner where the writers were found, where one could have ones letters written. The booksellers were also established there. A bit further on a quack tried to sell an ointment that — he claimed — could cure every disease. Attentively the audience listened to his explanation.

Quintus sniffed contemptuously. Oh yes, that fellow could tell a fine story but townspeople did not believe in this kind of talk. Perhaps a shepherd from the Campagna or a farmer from the province would believe this nonsense. Rome had exceptionally good doctors and if they could not cure you, then it would mean the end. Yet he was tempted to try out a pot. After all, it was not very expensive and perhaps it would cure his mother. She had been ill for over a year and was almost totally paralysed. But what was he worrying about! Davus, the coppersmith who lived next-door, had told him so often that such miraculous remedies did not exist. Irritably, he turned around and cleared his way through the bystanders.

After that he stopped briefly to watch a furniture-maker who was making a table out of lemonwood. But Quintus was not in the right frame of mind to wander around the market any longer so he took the road for home. He left the bazaar-street and entered the tangle of nameless, narrow, stuffy streets of which Rome had so many.

Here the poor of the city lived. The alleys stank and because the tenement houses rose five or even more storeys high on both sides, the sunlight never penetrated there. They were built with wooden frames, and slabs of dried clay served as bricks. As they were poorly built, they collapsed quite frequently. They were also very flammable. The ground floors of these buildings consisted mainly of workshops and warehouses, while above these, apartments had been constructed. In one of these "flats" Quintus and his mother had rented some small rooms.

He was home now. He entered the inner court through a gate. It was quiet there compared to the street where street-vendors, screaming children, and scolding mothers made a tremendous amount of noise. Yet, even here, there was quite some activity: the square resounded with the noise of hammer blows. Quintus smiled when he saw Davus, the old coppersmith, sitting in the shade of an awning.

"Hello Quintus," Davus greeted the boy as soon as he had spotted him. He stopped his work for a moment.

"Good afternoon, Davus. What are you making? Oh, I see, a breastplate."

The old man nodded his head while he shifted the small stone which he always kept in his mouth from the left to the right. His hand caressed the shining sheet of bronze that was lying on a wooden mould.

"Yes, I'm making a breast-plate for Centurion Julius of Augusta's cohort," he said, picking up his hammer again. "It must be finished by tomorrow because Julius has to wear it when he has to report to Caesar," he added, as if to apologise for continuing to work.

He usually took time off to have a chat with the boy who he had known from birth. Since the death of Quintus' father, he had acted more or less as his foster-father and Quintus did not mind this at all. He liked Davus.

With interest he watched the old man working. He had placed the sheet of bronze on a wooden block in which the exact shape of the breast-plate, complete with artistic decorations, had been cut. Using a small hammer, Davus beat on the back of the sheet, so that the bronze was driven into shape. From the front of the breastplate it appeared as if the figures had been made there. Davus was working on a small figure of the goddess Diana surrounded by a laurel wreath.

"May I try it on?" Quintus asked suddenly.

The coppersmith laughed. He took the armour off the wooden block and held it in front of the boy.

"It's almost the right size for you," he said.

"Well, I am sixteen already!"

"Yes, it is a pity that little children grow up so quickly."

"I don't think so. Oh, I would love to be a soldier myself," Quintus said when Davus put the harness back.

"Why?"

"Well, then you have the opportunity to travel through Africa, Egypt, Arabia, Armenia, Greece, Germany, Belgium, Britain, Gaul, Spain . . ."

"All right! I can hear you must have paid a lot of attention when the teacher told you where the borders of the vast Roman Empire are," Davus laughed. "But don't forget one thing: the barbarians who live at the other side of the borders know how to handle their weapons. Your father experienced that; he never returned from a battle in Britain."

Briefly Quintus' face clouded at the mention of his father.

"But isn't it good to die bravely and honourably?" he said pensively.

"Yes, of course, but this privilege isn't given to every Roman citizen, not even when he is a soldier. Don't be blinded by the prospect of wearing a handsome uniform and breastplate either. Military service is hard and not everybody can become a centurion or serve in the mounted cohorts. I know this from experience. For many years I was the coppersmith of the eighth regiment of the Batavian mounted cohort. I have wandered through the whole of the Empire — from the river Euphrates to the Rhine. I've seen miserable soldiers who had to walk for days on end, carrying their heavy packs. They arrived at the battle-field dead-tired where they had to fight well-equipped barbarians. Their death wasn't at all honourable or courageous. No! They were slaughtered like animals."

Staring off into the distance, Quintus did not reply. He imagined himself as a centurion, seated on a fiery war-horse and rushing over the battle-field. He did not even notice that Davus had started working again.

"Well, I'll go and see how Mother is," he said suddenly.

He rose from the low wooden bench and after having said goodbye to Davus, entered the house. Climbing a stone staircase he reached the second storey where he and his mother lived. An unpleasant, sour smell, caused by crowded living conditions, met him. Inside the house it was far from quiet. The many occupants created a lot of noise and the sound carried easily through the walls.

Quintus was home. A door on the dimly-lit landing led directly into the living-room, which also served as a dining-room and his mother's bedroom.

"Are you there, my boy?" a woman's weak voice asked as soon as Quintus had entered.

"Yes, Mother," he answered, going to the bed that stood in a corner of the room.

The woman on the bed showed every sign of having been ill for a long time. Her hollow cheeks were marked by the

19

pain she suffered and the lack of fresh air had made her very pale.

Quintus went over to the curtain that led out onto the small balcony. He opened them a little to let in some sunlight. Immediately the room brightened. Then he sat at the head of the bed.

"Did you have a good time, Quintus?" his mother asked.

"Oh yes, the games were terrific," he answered enthusiastically. "They again started with that Greek — you know, the one who fought the wild animals. This morning he won against two lions. What courage that man has, don't you think, Mother! All by himself, and armed only with a short dagger. He stood up against two of those savage beasts. It's already the fifth time that he has had a victory over them!"

It did not dawn on Quintus that a gladiator did not fight the lions because he was so brave. He was simply put into the arena and the animals were released. If he did not want to be torn to pieces he had to defend himself.

The sick woman nodded. "Yes, my boy, it must have been exciting to see a fight like that. I can still remember that from earlier days when your father and I went to the games.

"But now I have been in bed, paralysed, for two years," she added bitterly.

"How are you now, Mother?" Quintus asked, realising suddenly that he was only talking about his pleasure without thinking about his mother.

"Oh, not too bad," she answered. "But how I wish that I had the money to pay for a doctor. He could bleed me perhaps, and I might feel much better then."

"By the way, there's something I want to ask you," Quintus remembered. "In the street I heard that a senator Artotrogus has been ordered by Nero to have his veins opened. What does this mean?"

"Well, that means that he has fallen out of favour with the Emperor and according to his divine judgment has deserved death. Yet, being a friend of Nero, he does not have to die on the scaffold but, as a favour, can slash his wrists."

Quintus nodded to indicate that he understood. "Lately many of Nero's friends must have fallen out of favour," he said, "because I've heard this expression quite often but always forgot to ask what it meant."

"Yes, my boy, Emperor Nero is hard to please, but the divine Caesar knows what he is doing. We, ordinary people, don't always understand these things, but the gods do many things that are beyond our understanding. I made many sacrifices to goddess Fortuna and yet your father was killed in battle."

She sighed deeply and tried to change her position in bed. Quintus came forward to assist her.

"Shall we eat first?" he asked.

Without waiting for an answer, he stood up and went to the other corner of the room where a shelf was fastened to the wall. On it was food and a few simple pieces of crockery. It was dark in that corner. The opening to the balcony was the only source of light as the small room did not have windows.

"Do you want something to eat, Mother?" he asked.

"No thank you, I'll have some porridge tonight. Just give me a glass of diluted wine, please," she said listlessly.

Quintus poured the wine that his mother had asked for. He took some bread and a few dates from the shelf for himself. After he had helped his mother drink, he sat at the rough, wooden table and broke the bread into four pieces. He dipped a piece into a bowl of sauce and put it in his mouth.

"Did you have any visitors this morning?" he asked between mouthfuls.

"Yes, your uncle Scipio has been here," she answered with apparent reluctance.

The boy pricked up his ears. Since the death of his father, his uncle Scipio had been Quintus' guardian and had kept an eye on his mother. However, he only visited them when there was something special afoot. For the rest he was not very interested in his nephew and sister.

"Did he have any news?"

"Yes, he was talking about you," his mother said hesitantly, as if she did not dare to tell what had been discussed.

"What did he say then?" Quintus insisted.

"Well, he feels that a healthy boy like you should work."

"He has been saying that since I left school but I can't find anything suitable. Really, I'm always looking for work. Did you tell him that?"

"Yes, I did, but now Scipio has found a job for you."

"Where?"

"On the Aventine Hill with Aquila, the tentmaker. You are expected there tomorrow."

Quintus' face clouded over. Must he become a tentmaker? Surely that was not a trade for a strong boy? His dreams were shattered. Tentmaker! That was something entirely different from being a soldier or a centurion. If only it had been armourer or, at worst, coppersmith, like Davus. But tentmaker!!

Frowning, he stared off into the distance. Angrily he plucked off some bread and bolted it down. Yet he had to accept Scipio's decision. A guardian had the same rights as a father, and a father's will was law. That implied that a father was even allowed to kill his children when they transgressed his commandments.

Sulkily, Quintus cleared away the dishes. Without uttering a word, he withdrew himself into the small room that served as his bedroom. As was the custom in the south of the country, he took a rest in the afternoon while the sun was at its peak. Roughly he jerked the curtain across the opening.

Tentmaker! Whatever made his uncle think of that!

# Chapter 3

## *MAKING TENTS*

With her first rays the morning sun brushed playfully along the gilded, bronze shields that decorated the facades of the Basilica-Aemillia, the second largest building of the Forum. The biggest building was the Basilica Julia. In the colonnade it was still quiet. In a few hours time it would be different when the merchants would meet to do business. The Basilica would then serve as an exchange building. A division of the Vigilantes — night watchmen and fire-brigade — marched past on its way to the barracks.

This was always a sign that Rome was awakening. For a Roman the working day started at sunrise. This did not mean that during the night hours the city was quiet and deserted. On the contrary! During the night hours the transporters were doing their jobs because during the day it was impossible to drive through the streets. And it was forbidden. For that reason the market-halls were stocked up during the night. Bricks, for example, were delivered to the work sites for the many buildings being constructed in Rome. Toward the morning the heavy carts disappeared from the streets to make room for the crowds.

Some small groups of men were already on their way to work. They greeted the Vigilantes as well as some men dressed in white togas hurrying along the street. The latter were those who owed a rich man some money. They were obliged to report in white togas to the person to whom they owed the money and, with the rest of his employees, bring him the usual morning salutation.

Quintus, too, was among the workers. That morning he had set out early to go to the Aventine Hill to his first employer. As it was nearly an hour's walk, he left home at dawn. Arriving at the foot of the hill, he asked a passer-by for directions to the house of Aquila, the tentmaker.

"Oh, that's easy to find," he was told. "It is nearly at the top of the hill on the left hand side between two large houses."

Quintus thanked him for the information and continued on his way. Soon he reached the tentmaker's house where he let the knocker fall on the bronze plate of the front gate. Almost at once the gate was opened. He stated who he was and why he had come, after which the door-keeper asked him to come inside and wait.

It struck Quintus that the door-keeper was not tied by a chain, as was usually the case. In those days the door-keeper and his dog guarded the door; the dog was chained so why make an exception for the door-keeper? Therefore Quintus was surprised to see the guard walking about freely. Still, in Aquila's house he would see and hear more things that would amaze him.

The guard returned, accompanied by a middle-aged man whose features, despite the luxuriant beard, clearly showed that he was a Jew.

"Peace be with you," the man greeted Quintus.

"Lord, may the gods give you a long and healthy life and may you meet Lady Fortuna on your way," Quintus replied, and made his bow.

The Jew touched the boy's shoulder and said, "My name is Aquila; don't call me 'lord.' That's what a slave says to his master, and in this house there are no slaves."

That was something new! Quintus was astonished. In every well-to-do house in Rome there were slaves. Some noblemen possessed no less than four hundred and in a house like Aquila's one would expect at least fifty or sixty of them. All at once his thoughts went back to the guard who was not chained. Perhaps Aquila had been blessed so exceptionally well by the gods that he, out of thankfulness, had freed his slaves. Quintus followed his new master to the atrium, the largest main room of every private Roman house and the centre of daily activities. Several small rooms serving as bedrooms opened up into the atrium. The roof of the atrium sloped to the middle giving it the form of a square saucer. An opening had been made in the roof through which sunlight entered. During the rainy season, however, rainwater could run in freely and for that reason a pond was made right under the opening. The pond sometimes contained fish or selected water-plants, and it was surrounded by bronze or marble statues.

When Quintus entered the atrium the other labourers had already started work. Quintus counted at least twenty. Aquila walked with him to the edge of the pond and with a loud voice introduced the new servant to his fellow-workers.

"Have you ever made tents before?" his employer asked.

"No, Aquila."

"Well, then you have to learn this trade right from the start." Thoughtfully, the Jew looked about the room and rubbed his bent nose with his finger. "I think the best thing to do, is to help make a travelling-tent for Petronius. That's only a small job but all the tricks of the tent-maker's trade are involved."

Quintus followed him to a corner where a boy was working. As he approached, Quintus sized the boy up with his eyes. The boy looked about two years older than himself and seemed a decent chap. Being a true Roman who always paid extra attention to people's figures, Quintus was impressed by the athletic build of this muscular, young boy. To see such a fellow wrestle, clad only in a loin-cloth, so that his muscles stood out clearly, would be a magnificent sight, he reflected.

"Demas, this is Quintus," Aquila introduced him.

"Peace be with you," was Demas' greeting.

"By Hercules, may you have a long and healthy life," Quintus replied.

Soon after, the Jew left them by themselves and both boys started working. Demas explained what had to be done.

"We are making a travelling-tent for Petronius. We use leather, because leather is strong and can resist rain and sun as well as sandstorms. It's also light and easy to fold. We'll first select the leather and cut it into strips. We then sew them together to make the tent ready to try on the wooden frame that can be dismantled. I have already made that frame; look, it's over there."

Without interest Quintus nodded. He still was not enthusiastic about the tentmaking trade.

"Making a frame is really the most difficult part of the whole job, especially when you have to make a big one," Demas continued. "It should be strong and stable, as well as light and simple to take apart."

The boys had walked over to where the rolls of leather were stored. With an expert eye Demas selected the material. He lifted the heavy rolls as if they weighed nothing. With open admiration Quintus looked on.

"Are you a slave or a freeman?" he asked suddenly.

"A freeman! But why do you ask that?" Demas replied in surprise.

"Well, of course it's nice for you to be a freeman but on the other hand it's a pity. If you were a slave, we might have a chance of seeing you wrestle in the arena one day. What a beautiful strong body you have!"

Demas did not answer. His face set and he tightened his lips. It appeared to Quintus that Demas now lifted the rolls of leather with more vigour than was really necessary.

"We'll take this piece," Demas said abruptly. "Come with me and I'll teach you how to cut the strips."

The leather was spread out on the floor and with a piece of charcoal Demas drew the lines where it had to be cut. He told Quintus how to keep the leather tight and, taking a knife, he cut the leather in a perfectly straight line. Quintus, however, was more interested in the hand that handled the knife. With pleasure he looked at the swelling arm muscles. "I myself am no softie," he thought, "but this fellow definitely beats me!"

Without realising it, Quintus was sinning against the Lord. The Romans had adopted the Greecian ideas of glorification

of the body. The Greeks saw it from the point of art, but in general the Romans were not artistic at all and glorified the human body only at their sinful feasts and at the "games" in the arena. Both nations, however, forgot to honour the Creator of men. That is why Paul warned the Corinthians to consider their bodies to be temples of God.

Looking at Demas' arm, Quintus' thoughts wandered to the amphitheatre. What if such an arm handled a trident! It would surely poke right though the shield.

"Tell me, did you go to the games yesterday?" he asked Demas.

Annoyed, the boy shook his head.

"Then you've really missed something!"

Demas looked up. "Did I miss something because I didn't look at that slaughter? You've got to be joking! That spectacle is one of the greatest sins of the Roman nation," he snapped.

Quintus gasped with surprise. Completely puzzled, he stared at his work-mate who had continued cutting.

"Do you think the games are massacres?" he asked incredulously. It was the first time he had heard someone say that. He thought Demas must be out of his mind.

"What else could they be?" Demas asked and stopped cutting.

"It's an entirely honest fight," Quintus argued. "Both have equal chances, haven't they? Only the strongest, bravest, and deftest man wins!"

Demas muttered something. "Won't you ever open your eyes?" he suddenly burst out. "Do you still call that an honest fight? It's simply murder, and nothing else! And thousands of people come to look at that slaughter — just to enjoy themselves.

"What's wrong with you?" Quintus responded.

Demas looked at Quintus with compassion. "Oh yes, you poor blind people. You don't know any better. But I'll ask you a few questions; perhaps then your eyes will be opened. Just imagine that Aquila came to me and said, 'Demas, this afternoon, at 3 o'clock, you have to kill Quintus; here is a sword.' Would that be murder?"

"Of course," Quintus answered readily.

"Fine. But now Aquila also comes to you and says, 'At 3 o'clock you have to kill Demas; here is a trident.' Would that be murder?"

"Yes, I think so," Quintus answered, not quite understanding what Demas was driving at.

"Correct. And now Aquila goes to all his friends and acquaintances and invites them to watch this fight between us two. Can't you see that we then have the same situation as in the arena? There, too, the gladiators are charged to kill each other. And if you also bear in mind that God has commanded 'You shall not kill,' then you might understand that the Christians abhor the so-called 'games' and never attend."

"The Christians?" Quintus repeated. "You don't happen to be a Christian then?"

"Yes, I am, and I'm not the only one here. Nearly everybody in this house is a Christian."

"Well, well! And that's why you never go to the amphitheatre? You must be bored when you have a day off."

"Not at all. Quite the opposite. We can't imagine that other people go to the theatre just for their enjoyment. And, what is shown there is entirely against the command of the Lord Jesus Christ: 'You shall love the Lord above all and your neighbour as yourself.' That's completely different from enjoying yourself by watching the suffering and death of your fellow-men, isn't it?"

Quintus was just about to ask another question when a robust woman entered the atrium. She gave each labourer a mug of wine.

"That's Priscilla, Aquila's wife," Demas informed, while carrying on with cutting the leather.

The woman approached the boys. "Peace be with you," was her friendly greeting. Quintus looked at her and at the same moment knew he liked her.

"Good morning, Priscilla. May Vesta and Lars protect your life and home," he said getting up.

"Thank you, Quintus. May the grace of our Lord Jesus Christ work in your heart as well. Here you are, a mug of wine for you. It's ten o'clock, so you must be thirsty."

"What? Is it already ten o'clock, Priscilla?" Quintus was surprised. He could not imagine that time had passed so quickly. He was also puzzled about the serving of the mugs of wine and asked Priscilla about it. He had never heard of that before. Usually when the labourers were thirsty, they scooped up some water from the pond or fountain.

"As you did it to one of the least of my brethren, you did it to Me," the woman said.

However, for the boy they were incomprehensible words and sounded like a magic formula. Priscilla noticed this and explained the meaning of the words.

"Christ, the Son of God, loves all His people and it is His will that the people love each other, too. That's why He commanded us to do good to all people. He says that when you have done your neighbour a good turn out of love, then He regards this as having been done to Himself."

Quintus nodded but he hardly understood what Priscilla was talking about. A Roman did not know anything about doing good to a neighbour. He lacked regard for his fellow-man.

"Your uncle Scipio told me that your mother is rather ill. Is she all by herself, now that you are away the whole day?" she continued.

"Perhaps a neighbour will look in, but apart from that she never has any visitors," Quintus answered.

"That's terrible," Priscilla said sympathetically. "We will do something about that immediately. I can manage without one of the girls during the morning. Yes, I will send Cornelia; then at least she'll have some company and help," she said to herself. Turning to Quintus she asked, "What is wrong with your mother?"

"I don't know, Priscilla. The doctors who look after the poor are at their wits' end. They scratch their heads and disappear again. And we don't have money to consult other doctors."

"Oh, but that will soon be fixed, Quintus. I'll ask our neighbour Pudens to send their family doctor to your mother. He is a very wise doctor. He studied at the famous School of Medicine of Hippocrates, on the island Cos. With God's blessing he may cure your mother."

The woman left to carry out her promise.

"She seems a lovely woman," Quintus said after Priscilla had left.

"Yes, she is," Demas confirmed. He had listened silently to the conversation. "And what she is doing is showing love to her neighbour, just as she explained to you a minute ago. And don't forget," he added, laughingly, "she is the boss of this house. She is a woman who, with a laugh and a bit of fun, knows how to get her way. Yet, most of the time she's right. Often we are too easy-going or lazy, but she sets you to work."

The boys went on with their work and by noon all the strips of leather had been cut.

"Well, that was done quickly! We'd better have lunch first," Demas said with satisfaction. He stood up wearily and stretched his back, which had become stiff and painful from working in a bent position.

In the mean-time some pots with steaming-hot porridge made with wheat flour had been placed on the wooden table in the middle of the atrium. The workers drew up round the table with Aquila and Priscilla. Aquila prayed aloud the Lord's prayer.

Quintus did not quite know how to behave. The pagan Roman was totally unacquainted with prayers. What they — the pagans — always did, was to spill a few drops of wine as a sacrifice for the gods.

Demas noticed his embarrassment. "Just do as you are used to," he said, "That's what we are doing."

Quintus was thankful for this remark. He started eating as he was rather hungry. During the meal he had the opportunity to get to know his fellow-workers a bit better. Most of them had the slave-mark branded on their cheek. Quintus was surprised at that. Had not Aquila told him that there were no slaves in his house? He asked Demas about it.

"These slaves are freed men," Demas replied. "When, two years ago, the apostle Paul was acquitted by Nero, Aquila was so thankful that he gave all his slaves their freedom."

"The apostle Paul? Who's that?"

Demas shrugged his shoulders. "That's rather a long story," he said. "I'll tell you after the afternoon-rest."

Quintus continued his meal in silence. He was rather displeased with the delay but Demas seemed determined not to say another word about Paul during lunch. Stealthily, he looked around the table. Almost opposite him, sat a middle-aged man who, like Aquila, had a luxuriant beard. Quintus could not help looking at him, because every time the man put a spoonful of porridge into his mouth, it seemed as if a dark hole was opened. Later he learnt the reason for this strange appearance. Marcus — as he was called — had formerly been the slave of another master. This man had ordered to have Marcus' tongue cut out because, in his opinion, he had been insolent. This information did not surprise Quintus at all. People in Rome were used to that sort of thing. A slave was a thing, not a human being, and they should be treated harshly to teach them submissiveness and obedience.

After lunch everybody had a rest till the midday-heat had passed. Quintus, however, could not sleep. That morning he had heard so many things that now occupied his mind. There was Priscilla, a true Roman woman and yet full of care and compassion for her fellow-man. She seemed to be on very good terms with Pudens, the senator. Would he perhaps be a Christian, too? He must be, otherwise Quintus could not explain why such a high-placed person would have dealings with Aquila and Priscilla who were just ordinary members of the working class. Pudens had also made his family doctor available to treat mother. A doctor like him, coming from the School of Hippocrates, would cost a lot of money if you had to buy him for yourself. Such a valuable asset would not be lent out to just anybody. No, Quintus did not understand it at all. To him it was all topsy-turvy.

"You promised to tell me about that apostle Paul," Quintus said as soon as he was sitting with Demas at the canvas again.

The latter nodded, and after a short pause — as if to arrange his thoughts — he said, "The apostle Paul was in prison here in Rome from the year 60 till 62. All that time he lived in a room in the inner part of the city, not so far away from where you are now living. Although he was guarded by a soldier, he was free to receive visitors and we made thankful use of this opportunity. When people came to him, Paul didn't miss a single chance to talk about Christ."

At this point Quintus interrupted him.

"Perhaps you should first tell me who Christ is, then I may understand things somewhat better."

"Have you never heard of Christ?"

Quintus shook his head.

"Well, I mean Christ the Son of God."

"Of which god?" Quintus asked again, for pagan Rome knew more gods than one could count on ten fingers.

"Christ, the one and only Son of the Almighty God, who created heaven and earth."

"Oh, you mean Withra."

"No, I'm not talking about gods of stone or wood; they are idols made by men. I mean the only living God who is our Father in heaven. In the beginning He created heaven and earth and afterward He created men to live on the earth and to do this to His glory. But men wanted to be like God and rebelled against Him. Then God cursed the earth and punished men. They couldn't be on good terms with Him any longer, and they also lost the right to go to Him in heaven. God, however, is a God of love and that's why He gave mankind another chance. His Son, Jesus Christ, came to earth as a human being."

"Just like Jupiter and Mercurius," Quintus commented.

Demas ignored this remark and continued. "So Christ came to earth, in Judea, and preached that He wanted to pay God for the sins of the people so that they could go freely to God again, if only they believed in Him. To make up for the people's guilt, Jesus Christ offered Himself and died on the cross outside Jerusalem. This happened about thirty years ago."

Quintus was disappointed. "Do you believe in a God who let himself be nailed to a cross?" he called out in disbelief. "That's punishment for a slave! I've seen many die in that way."

Demas nodded. "You're right, Quintus. Jesus came to take our place and people are slaves, slaves of sin. God then said to Christ: 'Are You willing to become a slave to grant the people freedom? Then You will have to die like a slave too, on the cross.' "

"That will do. I know enough about that Christ," Quintus interrupted. "Now tell me more about Paul."

"As you wish." Demas continued, "Paul was an apostle of Christ. He travelled from city to city and country to country to tell the people about Jesus. He preached that there aren't numerous gods but that there is only One, and that by the death of Jesus the way to God was opened again for everyone who believes. The most glorious part of his message was that Jesus had conquered death. Three days after He died He rose again from the grave . . ."

"Like Attis."

"No, not like Attis. In the first place, Attis doesn't exist and in the second place — supposing he exists — he is so powerless that he by himself cannot rise out of the grave; priests have to assist the poor fellow. And what's more, nobody can recognise him anymore because he has changed into a pine-tree. Anybody can say: 'When I'm dead, I'll change myself into a pine tree.' Nobody can check that. Christ, on the other hand, was indeed identified. For forty days He presented himself to His disciples. Therefore the beautiful aspect of this Christian belief is that all those who believe in Jesus Christ are regarded by God as righteous through Jesus. This means that He adopts them as His children whose debts have been paid and who have conquered death."

"Okay, that's enough for now; my head is spinning," Quintus laughed. "I have no objections that you believe in that God and His Son. One God more or less in Rome doesn't matter!"

For the time being, the boys let the matter rest and continued their work in silence. Every now and then they exchanged a few words. Yet, Quintus could not help but look stealthily at the muscular arms of his workmate, but he did not make any remarks about them anymore. Toward sunset they stopped work. In a single file the workers walked past Aquila and his wife to greet them and receive their day's wages. To his big surprise, Quintus was given four sestertius, a day's wage for a qualified tradesman!

"A good worker is worth good wages," was Aquila's friendly remark.

Quintus looked at the coins in his hand. Had he really worked that well? By Diana! Making tents might be fun after all!

# Chapter 4

## *AFTER SUNSET*

With a relaxed mind, Quintus paid a quick visit to his old friend, the coppersmith. Already after the first visit of Pudens' family doctor his mother felt much better. The sick woman was also full of praise of Cornelia, who had been sent by Priscilla. She had attended to the patient very well, done some shopping and given the rooms a thorough clean. In the meantime she had chatted non-stop, so that Mother was very tired and wanted to go to sleep.

"You won't stay too long at Davus'?" she asked.

"No, I'll be back within an hour," he promised.

He walked down the stairs but when he came to Davus' room, he found that the old man was already in bed. Yet Quintus knew from experience that he was still welcome.

"Hello Davus! Already in Morpheus' arms?" Quintus joked.

"Well, not exactly in his arms yet, but he's already taken hold of my tunic. Come in, my boy, and close the curtain behind you. Attis hasn't been raised from the dead yet, so the evenings are still cold. Throw some more charcoal on the fire and light the lamp."

Having done this, Quintus sat on a stool next to the man's bed. The oil-lamp spread a soft, wavering light through the shabby room and the blaze in the coal basin radiated a pleasant warmth.

"How did it go today?" Davus asked, knowing very well that Quintus had come to tell him about his first working day.

"Excellent! Much better than I expected," he answered truthfully. "Making tents is more interesting than I thought it would be." He related in detail what had happened to him that day. At last he came to the point that actually had been his reason for visiting the old man.

"Davus, at Aquila's nearly everyone is a Christian. Perhaps you can tell me a bit more about them?"

Davus sat up quickly and moved the stone in his mouth from left to right. He leaned over toward Quintus.

"Christians, you say?" he asked, dropping his voice. "By Jupiter, don't have anything to do with them!"

"Why not?" Quintus asked, startled.

"Don't you know that? Quintus, they have such a terrible belief. They are common criminals!"

Sceptically, Quintus looked at the old man. "Criminals? I noticed nothing of the sort today. I just got the impression that they are doing a lot of good."

"Yes, yes, of course they have made you believe that. I've never heard a criminal testify of himself that he is bad. But you'd better believe old Davus. He has seen more of the world than you have. Just listen and judge for yourself. Do you ever see Christians at the games? No, you don't. And do you know why? They are against every form of entertainment. You also will never see Christians in the temples of our gods because they are the enemies of them. Just try to imagine that! Enemies of the gods who, throughout the ages, have looked after the Roman Empire. They won't even bring sacrifices to the divine Caesar; they don't want to honour Emperor Nero. Perhaps they even wish to dethrone him because they claim that the kingdom of their God will come on this earth and, of course, then Caesar must disappear first."

The old man paused for a moment to regain his breath. Dropping his voice even more so that Quintus had trouble hearing the whispered words, he continued.

"Do you know that at their secret meetings they drink the blood of sons of men? To be more exact: they kill small boys and drink their blood. They also say that the world will be destroyed by fire. Yes, you are surprised to hear that, aren't you? But it is understandable that they act like that, for their God is a hideous being. That's why in their houses you will never see a picture of Him. They are ashamed of Him because, despite having a human form, He has the head of a . . . donkey!"

Davus nodded his head emphatically to add weight to his words.

"I can hardly believe that what you are telling me is true. I didn't hear any of this today," Quintus objected.

"By Honor and Virtus, it's true, my boy! But now you know this, it won't do you much harm anymore because now you can oppose those who try to force their ideas upon you. There is still another reason why you have to avoid their houses. There is something that you cannot fight against. They practice witchcraft. Yes, it's true," he added when he saw Quintus look at him incredulously. "Listen. Centurion Julius, for whom I made that breast-plate yesterday, once told me a strange story. Four or five years ago he had to accompany a prisoner, a certain Paul, to Rome."

"Demas told me something about him just this afternoon," Quintus nodded.

"Well, that Paul, although he wasn't a sailor could predict if there was a storm coming. The captain of the ship didn't believe Paul of course. But the storm did come and all on the ship were dead-scared. Then Paul made another prediction. He said, 'The ship shall be wrecked but all those on board will be saved.' And it happened just as he said! But once on dry ground, an even stranger thing occurred. The castaways had made a fire on the beach to warm and dry themselves. Paul went to put an armful of branches on the fire, a poisonous snake came out of the bundle and bit him on his wrist. Naturally, everybody thought that Paul would die. But he wasn't the least bit hurt by it. By Pollux, I ask you: is that witchcraft or isn't it?"

Thoughtfully, Davus stared off into the distance. "Oh boy, if the gods ever hit Rome because of the misdeeds of the

Christians, you'd better hide yourself. You can be sure, that no sacrifice will be big enough to turn away that wrath!"

Deep in thought, Quintus returned home. Not for one moment did he doubt the words of the old coppersmith. Yet it was hard to imagine that Aquila, Priscilla, Demas, and all the others he had met that day, were capable of committing such horrible crimes. Could one be helpful and friendly and, at the same time, be an enemy of mankind? No, he did not know how to solve that problem. His thoughts went round in circles and he could not work it out.

When he arrived home, Quintus went to see if his mother still needed something, but she was asleep. That was the first time in weeks, for usually she lay awake for hours at night. Was this also witchcraft? He did not know. He wondered about these things as he filled up the oil-lamp and ate some dates before retiring to bed. Going to sleep quickly would be out of the question. He had too much on his mind.

Night descended upon the city.

The Vigilantes did their rounds and the night-workers started their duties. In the palaces of the rich, whips lashed the backs of slaves who, in their masters' opinion, had misbehaved that day. In the bakeries, slaves toiled at the heavy grindstones of the flourmill while others stoked the fire under the ovens. Tomorrow there had to be enough bread for the one and a half million inhabitants of Rome. A funeral procession wended its way down on the Via Appia. In those days the quiet of the night was often used to bury the dead. At another place a midwife left a house, carrying a new-born child. According to the Roman custom a child, after birth, was placed on the floor after which the father was called.

This was always a very tense moment. If the father picked up the child, it was accepted, but if he left it on the floor, it was rejected by him. Whatever happened to the child after that did not bother him. The baby being carried by the midwife had not been picked up by its father and she was taking the crying child through the dark streets of Rome. She would put it down in a sheltered place, leaving the child to its own fate. During the night somebody might find it. Perhaps it would be a man who would pick it up and regard it as his slave. Or somebody living nearby would be so annoyed with the crying that he or she would pick it up and throw it into the Tiber. If, however, nobody took care of the child, one of the many ravenous dogs that roamed the streets of Rome in search of something to eat, would certainly know what to do with it. Anyhow, by the next morning the child would have died of exposure to the cold and of hunger. It did not matter; the father had rejected it and so it was literally left to its own fate.

The night descended deeper upon the city. In most of the houses the occupants were asleep. At the Palatine Hill, in Nero's palace, however, it seemed as if the day had just begun. The luxurious, beautifully furnished marble palace stood bathed in a sea of light created by numerous oil-lamps placed on ornamental candlesticks. Fires in silver bowls were burning throughout the palace. Periodically slaves threw handfuls of incense on them. At the gate, illuminated by flares, the noblemen and patricians of Rome arrived one after another. The senators and the high officers of the legions with their retinue were also present.

Emperor Nero was having another of his famous, or rather, notorious night-parties.

Gradually, the guests filled the festive hall and reclined on the ivory couches that stood along the tables. All were wearing wreaths made of flowers and were dressed in their most colourful togas. The ladies were showing off expensive jewellery and competed with each other in wearing the most beautiful stoles. Their faces were heavily made-up with paint and powder, and their hair had been sprinkled with gold-dust.

The guests rose from the couches and cheered loudly when Nero entered the hall. He was accompanied by the Empress

Poppaea, an extremely beautiful woman with an unscrupulous and ferocious character. The pair seated themselves on a raised platform. With satisfaction Nero looked about the hall. Here, in the light of the oil-lamps, his face seemed even more cruel than it really was, and in his eyes one could already get a glimpse of the insanity with which he would suffer in later life. Although he was only twenty-seven years of age, he was obese. The red beard that he grew to mask his many chins gleamed as if it was made of copper.

Next to the Emperor were seated his trusty advisers: Seneca, Petronius, Rufus, Lucanus, Vespasianus, as well as Rome's most despicable man: Tigellinus. The Pretorians were stationed around the platform, because, even in the midst of his friends, Nero did not feel safe.

The banquet had started. Slaves walked to and fro with food and drinks. There was applause when some servants entered, carrying a silver dish with a peacock that had been roasted complete with its long tail. It seemed as if the bird was still alive. There was shouting and singing, and as more wine was poured out the guests became increasingly boisterous and exuberant. The jugglers and clowns had an appreciative audience. A couple of gladiators appeared and endeavoured to kill each other. The guests did not pay any attention to them; still, a feast in Rome could not be called a feast if there were no gladiators fighting. The dishes and delicacies served up received much more attention. Some guests were so sorry that they had already eaten and drunk their fill, that they took an emetic to induce vomiting. Then they could start eating again! Slaves dashed forward to clean up the filthy mess.

At one of the tables there was a sudden disturbance.

Britannicus had a heart-attack and died. He now lay slumped on the couch. Some servants quickly carried the deceased out of the hall. Nobody followed them because it was strictly forbidden to leave the party without a valid reason, and death was not an acceptable excuse according to Nero. He had seen so many deaths during his life. Had not he ordered to have his mother murdered? And he had even looked on when the soldiers at his command had thrust their swords into her belly. And what about Octavia, his first wife? She had been put to death because he wanted to marry Poppaea. Yet, these dead people did not leave Nero in peace. During the night their faces haunted him and he heard their whispering voices. Nero's conscience was very uneasy and gradually he was becoming insane. He sought distraction in violent and revolting scenes.

When the dead body of Britannicus was carried past Caesar, he did not even look up. He clapped his hands and at this order the purple curtains at the back of the hall opened to shouts of admiration.

The section of the hall behind the curtain had been magically transformed into an exotic garden in which Asian male and female slaves danced. This spectacle made everyone forget the sudden death of Britannicus. Many guests, including some women, were drunk. With burning faces they looked at the dancers. The heat of the oil-lamps, the odours of the Arabian fragrances, mixed with the sweaty smell and the stench of the vomit — which the slaves no longer cleaned up — made the air stuffy and uncomfortable. The wreaths of flowers around the flushed heads had withered or fallen down. Roses whirled down on the guests at regular intervals from an arrangement of nets in the ceiling. The rose-petals, which quickly withered and were tread upon, did not help to freshen the atmosphere in the hall. Somewhere in the room a woman complained about the heat. A man staggered toward her and while the hall rang with laughter he started to cool her down with large quantities of wine.

Nero was also totally inebriated. With drowsy eyes he looked at Poppaea.

"Listen Seneca," he then said with a thick tongue. "I've made a song about the fire of Troy. Do you want to hear it?"

The senator's answer was almost lost in the shouting of the others.

"Yes Caesar, let us enjoy your divine voice and your unparalleled poetic art."

Nero smiled and stood up, reaching for a lyre.

Shouts for silence were now heard. "Caesar is going to sing!" Revelers who had fallen asleep and were snoring loudly, were woken up quickly. If they did not wake up quickly enough, they were manoeuvered away under the tables. Gradually the noise faded away.

With much show, Nero tuned the instrument and started to sing. He regarded himself as a great singer and poet, even composing the music for his songs himself. With much feeling he sang the song about Troy's fire. Every now and then he had to swallow deeply to master his tears, but toward the end of the song they streamed down his fat cheeks.

The fire had been terrible! In the mean-time, however, Nero's eyes wandered around the hall to see if someone dared not to listen to his divine singing. Any poor fellow caught could be sure that a centurion with ten men would call on him the next day with the friendly order to have his wrists slashed speedily.

At last the song ended. Those present burst out in loud cheers, although most of them, if they were not too drunk, had realised that Nero had copied large parts from the epic poem by Homerus.

"Was it good?" Nero asked childishly.

The senators hastened to praise the song. "You have done even better than Homerus, oh shining morning star. How blessed we are to be allowed to live in the same time as such a great artist, and to hear from his own mouth these magnificent songs. Our poor descendants are to be pitied that they will

know your divine voice only from hearsay and will hear the songs recited by mere actors!"

Nero was extremely pleased. He considered his artistic gifts to be his greatest triumph and fancied himself to be better as a poet and singer than as an Emperor.

"Yet, something is lacking in my song," he complained.

Of course, the senators denied this emphatically.

"Yes, yes," he insisted. "You wouldn't have noticed it because of my dramatic recitation but when you quietly read my poem, you will agree that the burning city I was singing about is not real."

Somewhat sadly he looked ahead. Then he called out, rather angrily, "But how can I sing about a burning city when I have never seen one? Is there a city on fire somewhere? Tell me, and I'll go there immediately!"

The guests shook their heads. On this point nobody could help him.

"But promise me that you will tell me as soon as one is on fire," he pleaded.

"Yes Caesar, we will," they promised with one voice.

They all reclined on their couches again and raised their wine glasses. However, the feast was coming to an end. In the east a new day dawned. The morning star shone brightly. Or was it the eye of God who looked down at this wicked city? Then the rising, blood-red sun could definitely be compared with the red, tear-stained eye of Christ who wept about the sins of Rome's inhabitants.

If Davus had been a Christian, he might have said, "If God one day will hit Rome because of the misdeeds of the Romans, then only the sacrifice of Jesus Christ will be great enough to turn away God's wrath."

Nero's guests did not give this a thought. They let themselves be carried home in their palankeens to sleep off their intoxication. They needed to renew their strength for the next night feast at the Palatine Hill.

# CHAPTER 5

## *STRANGE EXPERIENCES*

The next morning Quintus and Demas set out early. They had to collect a parcel of canvas from a skipper whose ship was moored in the Tiber. On his shoulder Demas carried a set of poles that were joined by straps to form a stretcher. When the rolls of canvas were put on these poles they would be easy to carry. There was also some webbing fixed to the end of the poles, allowing them to carry the load on their shoulders with little effort.

Together they walked on. Demas was in a hurry because he wanted to be on his way back before the traffic became too heavy, and there was quite some distance to cover. Quintus wanted to talk about the conversation he had had with Davus the night before but he did not dare. The subject would not exactly please Demas, would it? At last, he could not keep silent any longer.

"Last night I heard strange things about the Christians," he started.

"That's quite possible," Demas answered. "When people do not understand something, they condemn it. And when they do not know precisely what's going on, they start to imagine things."

"They say that you people slaughter children and drink their blood."

Suddenly Demas stopped walking. For a moment it seemed as if he was going to laugh, but then his face set.

"Yes, I know," he snapped. And with a sigh he added, "Indeed, people talk such nonsense."

"I simply cannot imagine that it is true," Quintus quickly continued, intending to comfort his friend somewhat. "I thought the Christians always say: 'You shall not kill,' so there must be something amiss. On the other hand, there must be some ground for that claim. Old Davus who told me is definitely not a liar."

They moved on again while Demas explained how this myth might have been gained prominence.

"People have twisted the words that they have only partly heard and didn't understand," he said. "Jesus Christ called himself the Son of men. They changed it to 'sons of men,' and therefore 'little children.' Also, during the celebration of the Lord's Supper, a cup of wine is passed around after the Presbyter has said, 'This is My blood.' He quotes the words of Christ, who made wine the symbol of His blood."

Quintus nodded. "I see," he said.

Both occupied with their own thoughts, they continued on their way in silence. Every now and then they greeted a passer-by or some members of the Urbani — the police — as they did their rounds.

"Tell me," Quintus said suddenly, "I'm told that the Christians don't sacrifice to Roman gods."

Demas shook his head. "Of course not! I told you yesterday that there is only one God. How is it possible then to sacrifice to gods made by human hands?"

"No, that's true," Quintus conceded. "But what about making sacrifices to the Emperor? I can't believe that Caesar has been made by human hands," he said jokingly.

"Sacrifices and worshiping should only be directed to God and certainly not to a human being, not even when that person has exalted himself to be a god."

"So it's true that Christians are enemies of the Emperor?" Quintus asked. He shuddered when he thought of the consequences this could have.

"Not at all! Who told you that? Just because we do not acknowledge Nero to be a god, doesn't mean that we won't accept him as Emperor. The governing authorities have been established by God and the Christians are commanded to obey these authorities."

The boys had reached the river and started to look for the skipper.

"On Sunday night there will be a meeting at Aquila's. You'd better come along. Then many things will become much clearer to you," Demas invited his friend.

Quintus nodded in agreement. His eyes wandered over the yellowish, muddy water of the Tiber. It was mid-March and the rainy season was not quite over yet, so the water in the river was still at a reasonable level. During the summer months the river was often too shallow for navigation.

It was still quiet in the numerous hotels and inns on the quays. At night it was much busier, because the banks of the Tiber functioned as the centre of amusement for the common people. They held the same sort of parties there as did the rich in Nero's palace, though on a simpler scale. This was also the place to listen to the stories told by travellers and peddlers who stayed overnight in the inns.

There was plenty of activity at the hundreds of warehouses that stood along the banks of the Tiber. Labourers and slaves carried goods back and forth. The storage buildings had to be filled to capacity before the river became too low.

Quintus enjoyed the bustle, but Demas kept looking for the familiar ship from which he had collected canvas before.

"Look Quintus, there it is," he pointed to a flat boat. "There, behind that ship with cows and pigs."

"Oh yes, I see it."

Soon they had reached the boat. The skipper was sitting on deck, busy gulping down some porridge.

"Peace be to you, Stephani," Demas greeted.

"May Castor and Pollux bless and protect you and your ship," Quintus added.

"If I had to be dependent on Castor and Pollux, I wouldn't earn enough for my bread and cheese," the man muttered, "and never again will I moor at this place!" With his thumb he pointed over his shoulder to a boat loaded with blocks of marble and pepperstone. "Those fellows over there, have been busy the whole night. I didn't sleep a wink. All night I could hear the monotonous call: 'Hey, hup! Hey, hup!' To make matters worse, a cart collapsed because they tried to load it with a stone that was too heavy for it. Two slaves were crushed by it and the unfortunate fellows were thrown into the Tiber without much fuss."

The man continued to complain while helping the boys to secure the canvas on the stretcher.

"And during the day they don't leave you in peace either, Stephani," Quintus said, laughing. He pointed to the boat with cows and pigs, which was being unloaded by slaves. The shouts of the drovers were heard above the lowing of the cows and the squealing of the pigs. They had to drive the animals to the large halls where the cattle-markets were held. The boys and the skipper could not help watching them for a while.

"From what I see, those animals are treated better than men," the skipper grumbled. He had been a slave in the past.

Quintus did not even hear what the embittered man was complaining about. He kept staring at the cattle-boat.

"A pig has escaped!" he suddenly called out. "It's coming this way!"

"Catch the animal!" the skipper ordered. He was thinking of the terrible consequences this carelessness could have for his former companions.

The boys did not need any encouragement. Catching the pig was just up their alley. With the help of the skipper, they tried to obstruct the way for the loudly-squealing animal. The pig dashed forward blindly, to escape its shouting pursuers. Demas and Quintus leaning forward, legs wide apart, stood ready to grab the clumsy animal.

Demas saw the pig coming straight toward him and he had already stretched out his hands to catch it. But, at the last moment it turned to the left and shot through Quintus' legs. Quintus was not prepared for this at all. He lost his balance and fell forward. Wildly he grabbed for support and clutched at what he could, which was the pig's back. He wound his arms and legs firmly around the pig's belly. Right before his eyes the curly tail danced up and down. Yet, the animal did not intend to give up and raced on with the rider on its back. Loud cheering was heard along the quay. Demas split his sides laughing, and even the peevish skipper could not hide a smile.

Work in the storehouses stopped, while grinning workmen looked at the spectacle. But nobody gave a hand to catch the pig. Its pursuers could not move either because they had to laugh so much.

And so the strange combination raced along the Tiber. Quintus was practically the only one who was not amused with the situation. He was somewhat ashamed of the silly scene he was making. He did not dare to let go of the pig in fear of being brought rudely into contact with the sharp, uneven pavement. Meanwhile, the cattle-drovers had continued their chase and appeared to gain on the animal. It was tiring because of the load on its back. Yet it did not like to abandon its recently obtained freedom without striking a blow. Pressed hard, it made for the bank of the Tiber.

Quintus, who could not see what was happening because he was lying on the pig back to front, was not conscious of the impending danger. He was even beginning to enjoy the situation and laughed at the shouting drovers. And so, without warning and to his great astonishment, he toppled into the river with his mount. Recovering his breath, he came to the surface and swam a few aimless strokes. Four slaves jumped into the water and amid loud cheering, Quintus and the pig were pulled onto the edge.

Quintus did not wait to see what would happen next and hurried back to the boat, together with Demas who was still choking with laughter. Eventually Quintus too, had to laugh. "It's a pity that I couldn't see myself," he sniggered, as he set out, soaking wet, on the return journey through Rome's streets.

After attracting a lot of attention in the city's streets, the drenched Quintus still had to give an explanation at Aquila's.

Naturally, Aquila wanted to know the ins and outs of the event. He listened with a serious look on his face, but then, together with the other workmen, he burst out laughing. Being an upright Jew, even-though he was a Christian, he could not suppress his inborn abhorrence for pigs.

"You'd better get those clothes dry and have a good wash and perfume tonight in a public bath house," he said, wrinkling his nose demonstratively. "A smelly pig plus the stinking water of the Tiber; I can't think of a filthier combination!"

For Aquila the matter was settled and he withdrew into his office.

Quintus got rid of his wet tunic and amid great hilarity, hung the wet clothes on the outstretched arm of a statue at the edge of the pond. He dried himself with a woollen cloth and, clad only in a small loin-cloth, went to help Demas making the tent for Petronius.

Demas could not help looking with admiration at the muscular, lean body of his companion. "Dear me," he thought, "Quintus would match me in strength and agility." For a second a desire ran through him to measure his strength against that of Quintus. True, he was a Christian, but his old Roman pride about bodily strength and courage had not completely disappeared. During their return trip Quintus had teased him a little as well. While carrying the stretcher with canvas, they were able to assess what each was worth. No doubt, Demas was the stronger of the two. He had carried the load without visible effort and had walked on steadily. Quintus had been irritated by this and had challenged Demas to a wrestling bout. Jokingly, the latter had refused the challenge. However, when Quintus was sitting next to him, he thought about it again. Quintus seemed to feel his friend's sentiments. He stood up, placed his feet firmly on the ground slightly apart, and braced his biceps.

"Just feel, Demas, hard as iron!" He folded his arms over his expanded chest. "Do you dare?" he challenged.

Demas succumbed to the temptation.

"All right! After the midday-rest I'll teach you a sharp lesson," he consented.

Quintus smiled. He got what he wanted; a wrestling match with the strong Demas.

A quarter of an hour before the end of the usual resting-time, the two boys secretly went into the garden. They looked for a suitable spot and took off their tunics. According to the rules, they took up their positions facing each other. The fight started.

Some workers who had heard about the wrestling, joined them to witness the spectacle. And, indeed, it was worth watching the fight between these two strong boys with healthy, sun-tanned bodies. It was even more enjoyable because it was not a life-and-death struggle. The loser did not have to die.

Nearly all the men now went to the garden to watch. They encouraged both boys. Even Marcus uttered unintelligible cries. All the spectators thoroughly enjoyed the wrestling.

Well, who could blame them for once again having come under the spell of the fight which briefly revived their memories of the arena. Most of them had only recently become Christians and had turned their backs upon the amphitheatre. What harm could such a wrestling-bout between two boys do? Yet, the devil gained more hold over them than they themselves would admit. Some men made bets on who would win. No, they did not stake large amounts of money; just a few coins, or a piece of fruit but even in this the danger loomed that they might start to long for their former way of life. And the devil laughed. He had them firmer in his grip than they themselves realised.

Demas and Quintus continued fighting. Which of the two would win remained to be seen because the boys were well-matched. Although Demas was stronger than Quintus, he had not practised wrestling since the day he had become a Christian. Quintus, on the other hand, had been trained extremely well. Yet, who would eventually win was a question that was not to be answered!

Aquila was attracted by the noise, and suddenly appeared in the garden. He took in everything at a glance and immediately saw the danger. Eyes aflame and drawing himself up to his full height he thundered, "You ought to be ashamed of yourselves! Pagan wrestling in my garden, and that in the midst of Christians. Back to work at once! And you, pray to God that He may forgive your sin!"

Shocked and frightened, everyone sneaked back inside and continued their work. They realised that Aquila was right.

"Did I invite the devil too, when I took you into my house?" the Jew asked sadly when Quintus walked past him. Quintus did not answer and fastened his belt.

Without speaking he sat down next to an unhappy Demas who was bent over his work and did not dare to look up or around. Quintus shrugged his shoulders. He could not understand why such a great fuss was made about an innocent wrestle. It was a healthy activity. Quintus became annoyed. Davus had been right last night after all. Christians were enemies of every kind of amusement.

Upon arriving home at night, Quintus found his mother in an excellent mood.

"Hello Mother," he greeted. "How are you?"

"Very well, my son. The doctor sent by Priscilla must be a very clever man. Although he cannot guarantee that I will ever walk again, his prescribed medicines bring me much relief. For the first time in months I don't have a headache."

Quintus was glad with this improvement and placed the hot dinner he had collected from the common eating-house on the table. His mother, like many other Romans, did not have a kitchen at her disposal.

"You must be hungry then!" Quintus said.

"No, not at all. Cornelia looked after me so well this morning. What a darling she is! Nearly the whole morning she has been sitting at my bed and she couldn't stop telling me about a God named Christ."

"I'd rather you not mention that," Quintus requested. "At Aquila's they are all Christians and all day long I hear nothing else."

"Then you are fortunate to have found work with such nice people, I think. When I hear the stories Cornelia tells me and see what Priscilla does for us, Christians must be very helpful and generous to other people."

"Perhaps you're right," Quintus muttered, shrugging his shoulders, "but I think Christians are a bunch of spineless people!"

# CHAPTER 6

# *THE HOUSE-CONGREGATION AT AQUILA'S*

"Davus, may I borrow a lamp from you?"

The old coppersmith put down his tool and looked inquiringly at Quintus.

"What do you need a lamp for?"

"I have to go somewhere tonight," he answered evasively.

"So, you have to go somewhere. Where, if I may ask?"

"Oh, to a meeting of the Christians," Quintus said as lightheartedly possible.

Astonished, Davus nearly swallowed his little stone.

"You have to go to a meeting of the Christians? I thought those were kept secret."

"I've been invited!" The answer sounded somewhat proud.

For a moment the old man was speechless but then he said sadly, "It's pity that those people have influenced you so quickly, my son."

He shook his head and quietly gazed ahead. But then he grabbed Quintus by his shoulder and looked at him pleadingly. "My boy, listen to the wise advice of an old man. Don't involve yourself with those Christians. It will be your downfall! Do you know that they say that the world will be consumed by fire? Well, to make their words come true they have to light that fire themselves. And if you are seen in their company so often, and there is a fire, you too will be under suspicion. Don't forget that!"

Quintus shrugged his shoulders and said, "The longer I am with the Christians the more I get the impression that all those stories about them are lies."

"Well, is that your opinion?" Davus said slowly. But then, triumphantly, he asked, "Then why are their meetings held in secret?"

Quintus could not answer that question.

"I'm going to that meeting just to find out," he said having given the question some thought. "Perhaps tomorrow I can tell you more about it."

Sighing deeply, the coppersmith stood up to look for a lamp.

"Well, it's up to you; I've warned you," he added.

Suddenly he turned around. "Does your mother know about it?" He asked this, hoping it would dissuade the boy from going to the meeting.

"Mother doesn't mind at all. That girl Cornelia seems to have quite an influence over her."

Davus shook his head dejectedly. "Is that so! But if you don't want to listen . . . here is your lamp. It has just been filled so it will burn for about four hours."

"I'll only use it on the streets, so that's more than sufficient. Thank you very much!"

As Quintus left the workroom the old man stopped him. "Promise me that you will leave the meeting as soon as you discover something that clashes with the good morals of the Roman laws." He sounded very worried.

Giving his promise, the boy left quickly.

It had been dark for some time. It was overcast and fragments of clouds raced wildly along the sky. There was also a new moon, causing the narrow slums and alleys to be pitch-dark. Only occasionally the glimmer of a lamp could be seen as a pedestrian hurried along the streets.

Quintus was very pleased to have some light. At least now he could see where he was going. He could not help feeling a bit uptight. He was seldom outside at this hour. He was also very tense about what was awaiting him — the meeting with the Christians.

What truth would there be in the stories Davus had told him? The words of the old man had made a greater impression on him than he would care to admit. Actually he had to agree with Davus. Why were the meetings held in secret if there was nothing to hide? The more Quintus thought about it the less he could understand what had driven him to accept the invitation to be present at the house-congregation at Aquila's. Was it sheer curiosity or something else? He did not know. He hurried on, causing the lamp to sway heavily at every step he took. This made freakish shadows appear on the walls, giving him a fright at times.

Soon he reached an area of the city where it was much busier. Here the transport workers were going about their business and Quintus felt relieved at having more people and light around him. Carts, loaded with vegetables, fruit, flour, fish, wood, or bricks, and many more articles, were driven to and fro. The market halls and the building sites were again being supplied with the necessary goods.

While some carts were pulled by donkeys or horses most of them were drawn by slaves. Torch-bearers cared for the lighting. Quintus, who rarely saw this nightly activity, was fascinated and stopped for a while. This was rather dangerous, as he soon found out. He was nearly run over by a large four-wheeled Gaulish cart, called a Petorritum. A foreman who saw what happened, yelled at him. Quintus walked on anxiously. Even at night one was not safe in Rome's busy streets.

At last he reached the Aventine Hill and waited for Demas at the place agreed upon. The cold made him shiver despite the extra woolen tunic he had put on.

Occasionally people passed him in groups of two or three. They all walked in the direction of the tentmaker's house. As he was wondering if all of them were Christians, Demas also arrived.

"Peace be to you," Demas greeted.

"The same to you, but I'd prefer the blessing of Luna, the moon-goddess. I can't see a hand in front of my face," Quintus answered.

"Come along, and please, don't mention the names of those heathen gods tonight," Demas' voice came from the dark.

Quintus promised this and followed Demas up the hill.

Having arrived at Aquila's house, Demas let the knocker fall on the front-gate. Almost immediately a small barred hatch was opened.

"Who's there?" a man's voice asked.

"Demas, and I have Quintus with me."

"The password?"

"*Lumen mundi* (the light of the world)."

The hatch was closed, the bolts of the gate were pulled back and the gate opened.

The boys slipped inside.

"Peace be to you," was the mutual greeting.

Quintus was surprised at this reception, especially when inside the gate he noticed four robust gate-keepers. Was it necessary to act so mysteriously and carefully if nothing evil was planned? He asked Demas about it. The latter nodded understandingly and said, "Yes, it seems strange. Still, it's necessary. I'll tell you why. For ages the Jews have expected the Saviour, that is Christ. When He came to earth the greater part of the Jews didn't believe in Him. They thought He was a deceiver and a blasphemer who dared to claim that he was God's Son. That's why they demanded His death on the cross. They didn't realise that in that way a prophetic word had been fulfilled. But in the eyes of the so-called 'Jews of the Old Dispensation,' all those who accept Christ as their Redeemer and Saviour, are great sinners. And the latter do everything in their power to make the Christians' lives as miserable as possible. They would like to exterminate us, even here in Rome. Nearly all the slanderous talks about us Christians originate from those Jews. They also try to disturb our meetings and therefore these precautions."

The boys waited in the passage for the service in the atrium to start. More people continued to arrive and repeatedly the greeting "Peace be to you" was heard.

A large group of people was admitted, and Demas pointed out senator Pudens with his family and slaves. Quintus was very keen to be introduced to the man who — without any compensation — had sent his family doctor to his mother. He wanted to thank him personally, but the rich man shrugged his thanks off in a friendly manner.

"That's why we are on earth, my friend; to help our neighbours," he replied easily.

Meanwhile, Demas had joined some young people. He signalled to Quintus.

"May I introduce to you the two daughters of Pudens: Pudentia and Praxedes, and his two sons: Novatus and Timotheus. Also, the most important one, at least for me, Caecillia."

"Tell me about her," Quintus asked, because the girl whose name Demas just mentioned, appeared to be a slave-girl.

"I am the maid of Claudia, Pudens' wife," the girl answered.

"But not for long now!" Demas continued with pride. "As soon as I turn eighteen I'll marry Caecillia. I already have Pudens' consent."

"Well, well," Quintus was surprised. "I didn't know you were thinking of marrying soon. But I must say, you could have made a worse choice."

"Yes, how do you like it, Quintus?" Novatus laughed. "Demas snatches away the most beautiful slave-girl of our house. And Caecillia wants to go with him too! One would think she has a hard life with us."

"Of course I haven't; I'm only too happy to be a servant in a Christian family," the girl defended herself.

The boys grinned. Caecillia had let herself be riled again.

They left Demas and Caecillia alone. Pudentia and Praxedes were already talking to other girls so Quintus remained in the company of Pudens' two sons, but none of the three knew what to talk about. Quintus, therefore, made a remark about Claudia, the boys' mother.

"Your mother doesn't at all look like a Roman to me," he said. "She is so slim and has long hair and blue eyes."

"It didn't take you long to notice that," Timotheus answered. "No, she isn't a Roman; she comes from Britain."

"And how did she come here then?" Quintus wanted to know.

"Have you ever heard of the British king Caroctacus and his daughter Claudia?"

"No."

"Well, my father — as every good Roman — has been a soldier. As chief-centurion he had to go with a legion to Britain to fight there. After some time the battles were won, and King Caroctacus and his daughter were made prisoners of war and sent to Rome. Our father was appointed to be their guard. However, before the transport had reached Rome, the guard and the captured princess had fallen in love. When Emperor Claudius asked our father what he liked to have as a reward for his brave conduct, he answered that he wanted the princess as his wife."

"And he got her, as you can see," Novatus laughingly added.

Judging by the look on Quintus' face he clearly thought there was not a word of truth in the story.

"So you are actually royal children," he stated hesitantly.

"Yes, we are. Just ask Aquila or Demas."

At that moment Priscilla let them know that the service was about to start. The boys, who had been talking in the passage, moved to the atrium. Quintus did not recognise the tent-factory anymore. The room had been cleared and benches had been placed throughout the room. There were many visitors and not everyone could get a seat. Quintus saw Pudens leaning against a column and beside him a beggar was doing the same. Nearby, Claudia the princess, was seated next to an old slave woman who was covered in sores. Quintus could not believe his eyes! He thought that Pudens and his wife, being the richest and most important guests, should certainly be given a place of honour. Whispering, he asked Demas about it.

Demas answered him softly. "God doesn't make distinctions. We all are children of one Father and it doesn't matter if we are rich or poor, slave or freeman. God loves us all equally."

Solemn silence prevailed when the service started. Unconsciously, Quintus was influenced by the sacred atmosphere which transformed the atrium into an extraordinary room. Everyone realised that God was present.

Aquila stood behind a table at one end of the atrium. He prayed a short prayer and blessed the people present in the name of God the Father, and his Son Jesus Christ. After that they sang some hymns to the praise of God. As was usual in those days, some songs were written by the people themselves. They also sang in turns; the women would sing a song and then the men sang an answer. After the singing, Aquila led in prayer that was interrupted from time to time when the congregation said "Amen." Quintus heard Aquila pray for all the needs and distresses of the world. After the prayer Aquila read a part of a letter written some time ago by the apostle Paul to the congregation of Rome. Quintus was fascinated. He listened when somebody else explained and talked about the part of Scripture that had just been read. He heard things that were totally new to him. The preacher told of God's love for all men, but also of man's rejection of that love. They wanted to be God themselves, no longer dependent on their Father in heaven. They thought they could do without Him. Man wanted to be free. But this freedom was an illusion because before they realised it, they had become slaves of the devil. Every hour of the day man grieved God. Then God rejected the human race and closed heaven for them. God's curse had struck the earth.

Quintus understood the last sentence very well. The heathen gods did nothing else than strike people with their curses.

The preacher went on. God had compassion on men; He still loved them. And by His love, men have an opportunity to set things right again. Man was allowed to atone for his sin. But alas! The sin was too great; no man can pay for it. Then Christ, God's only Son, offered to carry the punishment instead of men, and He was able to do this. Therefore Christ came to earth as a Man to bear God's punishment as a human being. After He had suffered, died, and risen from the dead, God His Father declared, "I consider Christ to be as Man and therefore, I can consider man to be as Christ. Christ has carried the punishment for sin and is My Child. In Him men have paid for their evil and have become My children. They may again come to Me in heaven where they can live without pain, trouble, or sorrow. In heaven it will be like it was in Paradise, before the fall into sin."

The preacher then earnestly urged the congregation to love God Who had done so much for them, and to show their love in trying to do God's will now, in this earthly life.

The sermon had ended. A strange feeling came over Quintus. He could not explain what it was but it was just as if he had been touched by something. He felt happy but also frightened.

The congregation sang a few more hymns while they all walked to the table at the other end of the atrium. Everyone carried something: bread, fruit, wine, flour, or money. It was all collected by the deacons who were standing at the table.

"What are they going to do with it?" Quintus whispered to Demas.

"It will be distributed among the poor and sick. With us nobody has to suffer want. The ones who have abundance, give for those who have shortage."

Then an elder approached Quintus.

"Have you been baptised?" he asked.

Demas answered for him and shook his head. "No, not yet, Phlegon."

"Then you have to leave, my son. We are going to celebrate the Holy Supper."

Reluctantly, Quintus complied with the request. He would have loved to stay a bit longer in these sacred surroundings where all the people were kind to their fellowmen. Yet, there was nothing he could do about it. The rule was that only baptised people could be present when the Holy Supper was celebrated.

Quintus left, along with some other men and women.

"Do you have to go to Trastevere, too?" one of the men asked him, as soon as they were outside.

"No, but I'm heading in that direction," Quintus answered, glad to have some company.

Together they walked along the dark streets. It was raining a little, and this made the sky even darker. Their conversation revolved around the sermon. The people were so impressed by it they could not talk about anything else. Quintus joined in too. He had listened to the sermon attentively but as yet many things were not clear to him. His companions, however, could answer many of his questions clearly.

All too soon for Quintus' liking, they reached the Porticus Margartaria. Here he had to turn left. Their parting words were, "Peace be to you."


Quintus continued on his way through the dark alley, pondering on the God of the Christians who was so totally different from the gods of Rome. The latter were only interested in their own desires. They would never sacrifice their lives to save other people. They would not even be willing to suffer some pain for them. That Christ and God were exalted beings Quintus understood quite well. They did not sin, which was a contrast with the heathen gods, who did the same as man did. The myths were full of stories about gods who had murdered another god, or who were married to another god's wife. Some were even married to their sister or mother. No, Christ was totally different.

The seed of faith had fallen in Quintus' heart. It had not yet grown into a strong plant but things had come to a point where he felt admiration for God, and understood that the Roman gods were far inferior to Him. Later, that admiration would change into reverence.

Yet, the devil was still active and did not intend to let go of his victim without any struggle.

"Why were only baptised people allowed to be present at the celebration of the Holy Supper?" Quintus asked himself suddenly. Nothing special happened there? Or, did there? Why were strangers not allowed to see what occurred?

He then remembered that he had seen a young woman with a small boy on her lap, sitting in front of him. Perhaps it was true that children were slaughtered! Was that small, happy toddler already dead and were the Christians now drinking his blood? The explanation Demas had given him the other day, could be a lie after all.

"Oh, that's nonsense," he pleaded with himself in protest. But the devil asked, "Are you sure about that, Quintus? Why did the unbaptised people have to leave when the Supper was celebrated? It was because something would happen that could not be done publicly. Yes, yes, the meetings of the Christians are more mysterious than one would think. The old Davus is right. Beware of those people!"

With conflicting thoughts, Quintus arrived home. After having checked if his mother was all right — she was asleep — he went to bed. All kinds of thoughts were spinning through his head. His thoughts centred on Jesus' death on the cross. Actually, was not it rather cowardly to surrender without striking a blow. Quintus' Roman nature, that liked revenge and fight, rebelled against that attitude. At least it was honourable to go down fighting. But to let yourself be led to the slaughter like a lamb; no, he could not appreciate that. Jesus was not the obvious god for the Romans, he thought. Christ would make all the people cowards.

Suddenly he jumped up. Of course, that was the Christians' whole plan! If the Romans became cowards, then they would not dare to fight their enemies any longer. The whole Roman Empire would collapse like a house of cards. And then . . . yes, then the kingdom of that Christ could come. Of course! That is how it would happen. It was silly of him not to have thought of that before!

However, some time later he also remembered parts of the sermon which spoke of totally different things. Quintus was frustrated. Worn out, he finally fell asleep.

# CHAPTER 7

# *ROME ON FIRE!*

Quintus had now been working at Aquila's tent factory for four months. Contrary to his initial expectation, he enjoyed working there and took pleasure in the trade. Aquila noticed this too, and encouraged him to put even more effort into his work. But what the Jew liked best was the interest Quintus showed in the faith of the Christians.

Not that Quintus had become a Christian yet; far from it. It was Quintus' opinion that Christians were forbidden too many things, and exactly those things that made life bright and pleasant. God in heaven might be good and full of love but He forgot that His followers on earth wanted to enjoy life as well.

Aquila and the others disputed this fervently. "God doesn't forbid us anything," Aquila said. "God only commands. That's why we say the 'ten commandments' and not 'the ten prohibitions.' If you study them properly, you will realise that the ten commandments make life on earth bearable. Without the law it would be hell on earth. For then everyone could steal, kill, commit adultery, lie, and deceive to his heart's content. Really Quintus, God looks upon us with favour. And if you truly love God, you can do nothing but keep His commandments."

Although Quintus could not agree with all that was said, Christianity had already had some influence upon him. For instance, he had changed his view on the games, but on the whole he remained hesitant.

That is how Quintus' thoughts had developed. It was the morning of the nineteenth day of July, A.D. 64. He had been sent on an errand to the country-house of Hermes, about four kilometres outside Rome. Hermes was one of the most important characters in the first Christian congregation at Rome. Quintus had brought several messages from Aquila to him before.

He walked briskly because he wanted to reach Porta Capena as soon as possible and leave the city's stinking, narrow streets behind him. It was still early in the morning, but it was already sweltering. The heat built up between the houses. Household waste and open drains spread a choking stench. Perhaps at the Via Appia it might be more bearable, he thought, although there it also would be very unpleasant in the burning hot sun. The dust on the road whirled up with each step and penetrated everything.

Once outside the city, it did not take long for Quintus to realise that even here it was not much better. Now he understood why the couriers, who often had to walk or ride the country-roads, always wore large hats with very wide brims. The sun burnt his head. He looked at the fountains and water-basins in the gardens of the country-houses along the road and wished he could cool down there for a moment!

At last he reached the tomb of Calixtus and turned left toward a small valley. The country-house of Hermes was situated at the bottom of this valley. About ten minutes later, and sighing with relief, Quintus let the knocker fall on the front gate. Sestianus, the doorkeeper, opened the gate. The man was not chained and joyfully welcomed Quintus. He knew Quintus well from earlier visits.

"Come inside quickly; it's nice and cool here," he invited heartily.

After having washed his feet and straightened his tunic, he followed Sestianus to the atrium. "Hermes is in the Peristylium, the garden room," he informed.

In the atrium, Quintus, as usual, stopped to look at the magnificent wall-painting representing Solomon's judgment.

"Beautiful, isn't it?" he said softly.

"Yes, indeed, but I prefer the painting of the Sower."

"I haven't seen that one, but I did see the one with the bunches of grapes," Quintus answered.

"There may be time afterward to look at the ceiling painting," Sestianus promised.

They walked through to the Peristylium. Quintus had not been here before. He stared at this magnificent garden that was surrounded by a covered portico, which led to several rooms. The sun was shining on the most exotic flowers Quintus had ever seen, and made the waterdroplets of the small fountain sparkle like diamonds. Old Hermes was sitting in a summer-house, sheltered from the sun.

"Peace be to you, Hermes," Quintus greeted.

The old man bent his head forward a little to see who was standing in front of him.

"It's Quintus. He's been sent by Aquila," Sestianus informed him.

"I've a letter for you, Hermes," Quintus said rather loudly because the gray-haired man's hearing was not too good.

"Oh, thank you. Do you have to wait for an answer?"

"No, Hermes."

"All right then, my son. Give my regards to Aquila and Priscilla, will you?"

Quintus made his bow and was about to leave when the old man stopped him.

"Ah, yes, Sestianus, it's better that the boy stays here till the midday-rest. It will be really too hot now on the road."

"Thank you very much, Hermes." Quintus was happy. Walking back in this heat did not appeal to him at all.

Hermes smiled and beckoned with his hand that they could leave now.

The door-keeper brought Quintus to the apartments of the servants. He gave him some food and drink, after which they talked for a while. Most of the servants knew Quintus well and questioned him about the latest news from the city. Sestianus, however, had become a special friend of Quintus. The man was also a Christian and a presbyter (elder) in one of the many house-congregations. What he appreciated most was that the door-keeper never talked about his faith.

"I don't think that it is necessary," he answered when Quintus made a remark about it. "I suppose you hear enough about Christianity at the tent factory."

"More than enough!" Quintus exclaimed.

"That's what I thought, too. You can overdo it."

"I wish Demas realised that," Quintus sighed. "He doesn't talk about anything else. His faith even comes before Caecillia!"

"But that's how it should be, Quintus. Christ Himself has said: 'anyone who loves his father or mother more than me is not worthy of me.' So don't blame Demas for talking so much about his faith. Did you notice, how much support he gets from it? It dominates all his actions. Demas is a true Roman and by nature a hothead. But because of his faith, he knows how to control himself, even though it demands a lot of effort."

"Yes, I've noticed that during the past months," Quintus agreed, thinking about his first days at Aquila's when Demas had tossed the rolls of canvas around after he had mentioned the arena. It had frequently struck him that Demas found it difficult to control his quick temper. He also knew that his friend struggled with his desire for revenge, so characteristic of a Roman.

"Then the Christian faith must have great strength to be able to influence one's character," he thought aloud.

"Yes it has! . . . But now, come with me, Quintus. I still have to show you the ceiling-painting of *The Sower*."

They stood up and walked to the room. When they had returned most of the servants were resting because it was the time for the midday-rest. Sestianus and Quintus soon followed their example.

Their rest was suddenly and cruelly disturbed by loud and persistent knocking at the front-gate. Sighing, Sestianus got up to see what was going on. A moment later, shocked and frightened, he was back.

"Rome is on fire!" he shouted.

Hearing this alarming news, all flew to their feet. They all shouted at once and wanted to know more details but Sestianus could not answer all the questions he was asked. He had opened the door to the messenger and the man, hurrying to Hermes' room, had only told him that a large part of the city was on fire.

"Where exactly?" Quintus wanted to know, becoming very worried about his mother.

"Somewhere in the vicinity of Circus Maximum. That's all I know."

"That's still some distance from where we live," Quintus said with relief. "But I'd better go home as soon as possible. My mother can't walk and you never know what could happen."

"Quite right, my friend," Sestianus nodded. "The Lord be with you."

As soon as Quintus walked outside he saw clouds of black smoke drifting above the city. It must be a big fire. He hurried to the Via Appia. When he had reached it, he was still at least three quarters of an hour away from the city gate. He kept his eyes fixed on the clouds of smoke.

It appeared as if the fire was indeed raging in the vicinity of the great amphitheatre. Well, then his mother was not in danger as yet. Before it had reached their street, it should have been put out. The Romans were experienced in fighting big fires. Frequently the flammable houses of wood and dried clay caught fire in the densely populated city.

When he arrived at the Via Appia he had a better view of Rome. He now realised that the fire was much bigger than he had originally thought. The amount of smoke increased every minute. Flames could be seen quite clearly. Then he met the first people who were fleeing from the fire.

"Where exactly is the fire?" he called out to them.

Most of them pretended they had not heard the question and walked on. One, however, stopped in his tracks. Terrified the man looked back as if he feared to be overtaken by the fire.

"Between the Caesar and the Palatine, right behind Circus Maximum."

The man hurried on. Quintus also, walked on quickly.

The number of fleeing people increased and rapidly grew into a steady stream. Hardly any of them carried luggage. They must have been surprised by the fire and had not found time to save anything, Quintus thought. Every now and then people called to him to turn back but he shook his head and, stubbornly, walked even quicker. The crowd became very dense. He could only proceed with the utmost of difficulty. He yelled and pushed but nobody seemed to care. His anxiety rose as he noticed that the fire was spreading rapidly. By Jupiter, if it went on at this speed, half of Rome would be incinerated before he had reached the Porta Capena. The thought of what could happen to his paralyzed mother made him struggle against the stream of people even more forcefully. He was now walking on the extreme edge of the road and still had trouble making progress. From fragments of nervous conversations he overheard, he understood that the district of Trastevere had already been reduced to ashes. But how was this possible if it was only an ordinary fire? Was not anybody fighting the fire? Even here the smell of smoke and fire was very noticeable.

"You'd better go back, Boy. You can't enter the city anymore," somebody called out to him.

"My mother is there," Quintus called back without looking up.

Grimly he pushed on. At last he was within a few hundred metres of the city's gate. Here he could feel the heat of the enormous fire and the pungent smoke made his eyes water and his breathing difficult. The crackling of the flames could be heard clearly. The fire was now only some blocks away.

Not knowing what to do, Quintus stopped. He realised that it was impossible to enter the city by the gate. Dense crowds of people squeezed through the narrow passage. Even a dog would not have a chance, Quintus had to admit. He saw how a young woman became jammed between the bars of the gate but the crowd, thinking only of self-preservation, pushed on. Powerless, he had to look on as the woman was squeezed to death. Briefly he saw the panic-stricken, bulging eyes in her ashen-gray face. Then the woman sank away in the sea of people and was blindly trampled under foot. Indeed, it was absolutely impossible to bring the crowd to a stop. All were driven on by the people behind them.

Quintus understood that he had to find another way to enter Rome. It appeared that the Via Nova was not yet on fire. If he could reach that road he would be able to save his mother. Suddenly he remembered an opening in the decayed wall around the city that he had used in his school days. It would be just big enough to squeeze through. He should have thought of that before!

Quickly he headed off to the left, and searched for the opening. His eyes were watering because of the smoke and he used his hand to wipe them. Soon he had reached the opening. He forced his way through it and was inside the city.

But, the chaos here was even bigger than at the city's gate. In wild panic the people crowded the streets. The only aim of poor and rich alike was to save their own lives. A few who had been able to save some of their humble possessions, carried their load on their back, but this only caused more trouble for them. Most of them got rid of their baggage, leaving it as an obstacle for others. It was soon trampled upon and reduced to rubbish.

The strongest men elbowed their way through while others carried sick relatives or friends. People called for lost family members and children cried because they could not find their parents. Cows and pigs that had broken loose from the market-halls and butcheries, zigzagged through the fleeing people. A mad bull killed several people among the crowd before a Pretorian could kill it with his lance.

Slaves took advantage of the total confusion and escaped from their masters' houses. The thirst for revenge was evident on their faces. They did not feel pity for others; nobody had ever shown any pity on them. Houses which had been abandoned by the occupants, were looted for money and valuables, and nobody lifted a finger to stop it. Here and there a division of the Pretorians and the Urbani tried to restore order but it was a hopeless task.

With difficulty, Quintus struggled through the streets, trying to reach his home. Time and again he came across burning blocks of houses which forced him to go back and change his route. The stinging smoke and scorching heat made breathing difficult. The roaring of the flames and the screaming of the people dazed him. He did not even notice that he continually bumped into others or that he was roughly pushed aside. He was obsessed by the desire to save his mother.

He no longer had a clear idea of where the fire was raging. Like a roaring monster the fire spread so quickly that blocks of houses that Quintus had passed only a moment ago, were suddenly ablaze from top to bottom. The enormous sea of fire drew such a large quantity of oxygen from the air that, every now and then, a gale blew in the narrow streets. Here and there a wall collapsed. The people who were buried by the burning-hot rubble screamed in terror but nobody cared about them. Everybody had only one aim in mind: to get away from this all-consuming sheet of fire!

Meanwhile the fire kept spreading. Circus Maximum, which could seat a hundred and fifty thousand spectators, had already been completely destroyed. The beautiful temple of Honor and Virtus had become one big pile of burning marble. The Carinae and the districts around the Palatine were in flames. Trastevere was a smoking ash-heap.

At last Quintus reached the Forum. It was still undamaged but it would only take a few minutes before all these beautiful buildings would fall prey to the flames. The stately temple of Jupiter Stator was already enveloped in an impenetrable curtain of smoke.

At the large square the boy rested for a moment. He coughed and rubbed his painfully smarting eyes. His hair was singed and the skin of his face was tightly drawn. Whirling sparks had blistered some parts of his body. Surprisingly, a fountain in the middle of the square was still spurting water. Quintus drank deeply from it, and then soaked himself thoroughly. Ah, that made him feel better!

Still, he had to go on; he was not home yet. He could not possibly tell how long it had taken him to reach the Forum. He had lost all notion of time. Nor did he have any idea at what speed the fire was spreading.

Quintus tried to look through the dense smoke to see where the fire was. To his horror it was much closer than he expected it to be. From where he was standing it looked as if the street of the bazaars — the Porticus Margaritaria — was already ablaze. If that were true, he was too late! Within minutes the fire would have attacked his house.

Despairingly he raced on through the already deserted streets. He was almost convinced that he would not make it. He would be too late! His mother would burn to death. He did not dare count on the help of the neighbours.

Was there nobody? They always said that the God of the Christians was very mighty. He had even saved Daniel's friends from the burning oven. Yes, the God of the Christians. Perhaps He could come to the rescue. And in his extreme distress, Quintus — for the first time in his life — prayed to God.

He still raced on but no longer met any people. Everyone had already sought safety. In this part of the city the fire had not taken them by surprise and therefore the flight had been more orderly. Perhaps people might still have found time to take his mother with them, Quintus thought. He stopped. Then it was not really necessary to be in such a hurry. In the suffocating atmosphere of heat and smoke he gasped for breath. Some people who had waited with their flight until they could not put it off any longer came toward Quintus. Now the fire had forced them from their houses. To his joy, Quintus recognised one of them to be his neighbour. He ran toward him.

"Have you heard anything about my mother?"

The little group of people stopped walking and looked at him. At first they did not recognise the boy with the singed hair, bright-red face and swollen eyes. But one of them rubbed the tears out of his eyes and then called out, "By Mars, it's Quintus!"

"Quintus? I've seen his mother," another said.

"Where? Is she still alive? Is she safe?"

"You're asking me something I don't know, my boy. I last saw her about five minutes ago. Old Davus was carrying her on his back."

Quintus did not wait for further information and raced on. There was still hope. Well, if his mother was still alive, then the God of the Christians could be assured that he, Quintus, would become one of His most faithful followers.

But, a few hundred metres further on he started to doubt again. Davus was old and certainly could not carry the sick woman for long. Would he able to walk quickly enough? The fire might overtake them.

Torn between hope and fear, Quintus walked on, but the rests he needed to get his breath back became more frequent. The hellish race through the burning city had taxed his strength. He was exhausted. It seemed as if his eyes were scorched out of his head and he could hardly see a thing. The heat increased as he advanced but the smoke was less dense close to the fire. Another three or four streets and he would be home.

Suddenly he tripped over a man lying on the street. Quintus muttered something and was already scrambling to his feet when his stinging eyes recognised the man. It was Davus!

"Davus! Davus!" he shouted hoarsely.

The old man lifted his head. Quintus saw that he had a large head wound, most probably received when something had collapsed on him.

"Quintus, my boy," the coppersmith said in a feeble voice, and tried to smile.

"Where is my mother?"

"Here . . . around . . . the . . . corner. Quick, Quintus . . . The words were barely audible. However, Quintus was already rising and running off in the indicated direction. Quick! Davus had said. He turned the corner but immediately shrank back. The street was already ablaze and a scorching heat singed his eyelashes. The hot air burnt his lungs and his temples throbbed as if his blood was boiling.

It was impossible to continue. He was forced to retreat. He stared blankly at the wall of fire. A dry sob rose in his throat, "Mother!"

Totally shattered, he stumbled back, driven on by that dreadful fire.

Returning to Davus, he knelt down.

"Fire everywhere! I can't get through any more," he cried.

The old man tried to put his hand on the boy's shoulder to comfort him but he lacked the strength.

"I . . . carried . . . your . . . mother. Everyone . . . had gone head . . . Wanted . . . help." The coppersmith's voice became an unintelligible whisper. Sitting on the street Quintus laid the injured head of his old friend on his knee. He was unaware that the fire could reach him any moment. He was totally disoriented. It seemed as if Davus once again wanted to say something but his face stiffened and Quintus understood that the man had died. The fire of Rome had robbed him of the two persons whom he loved most. He, with hundreds of others had suffered the same sorrowful plight on this dreadful day.

Suddenly Quintus jumped to his feet.

"And what do You have to say now, God of the Christians!" he shouted hoarsely. "If You are going to put things right, then punish those who are responsible for this mad fire!"

He cast a last glance at the body of Davus and stumbled away. He knew that he now had to get out of the city quickly.

# CHAPTER 8

## *NERO*

During the hot summer-months, Emperor Nero retreated to his beach-house at Antium, a coastal town. Although close to Rome, it was more comfortable there. It was cooler and there was no smell. Already early in spring, the imperial family had left Rome together with the court, special friends, their families and trains of slaves. An exodus like that was always a colourful sight, and half of Rome turned out to see the departure.

Nero, therefore, was not in Rome when the fire started. He was having a walk in the garden with his special friends, Petronius and Seneca, when a messenger informed him of the disaster. A faint smile played about his lips.

"Splendid!" he said.

The messenger's face clearly showed traces of the appalling things he had seen. He thought that Nero had misunderstood him or had underrated the extent of the calamity.

"Oh mighty Caesar, there are numerous victims. Many people were caught by the fire, and unable to flee and were burnt alive. Others have been trampled underfoot because of the panic. Still others have been buried under collapsing walls."

Nero, however, waved his hand. He glanced upward as if seeing a vision and said, "What does that matter? I shall rebuild Rome. It will have wide streets and spacious squares and there probably won't be room for all who lived yesterday. The fire will have a dual purpose in making room for the new Rome."

For a moment the Emperor continued to stare upward. Then he turned to Petronius and Seneca who, like the courier, were terrified when they heard Nero's abominable words.

"What do you think, gentlemen? Will I still be in time to see the fire while it is burning at its fiercest?"

Unable to speak, the senators nodded.

"Now, at last, I can finish my song about the burning city," Nero said softly, smiling to himself.

Suddenly he turned again to the senators. "My song will be even better than that of Homerus. It will be realistic because I'll make it while I watch the city burning in front of me! A burning city! Old, stinking Rome is burning! Ha, ha! It's burning for me. For me only! Do you hear that?!"

Nero had screamed the last sentences. Laughing insanely, he crossed the garden toward the palace with long strides. "Harness the horses to the carriage! Rome is burning and I must see it!" he roared from afar.

Petronius and Seneca looked at each other, as they followed their emperor at a distance. Their faces were pale.

"This is the beginning of the end," Seneca said, shaking his head sadly.

"Unfortunately, you are right," Petronius sighed. "Indeed, this is only the beginning but where will it end?"

Toward nightfall Nero and his retinue of noblemen and senators arrived at his palace on the Palatine hill. Tigellinus came to greet him.

"I salute you, oh divine Caesar, son of the mighty gods. I hope everything will meet your divine requirements."

The Emperor nodded affably.

"More than that, my dear Tigellinus. It's magnificent!" he called out excitedly. "What's your opinion? Is it dark enough yet to get an impression of the fire?" he added impatiently.

The company went to the roof of the palace to get a good view of the fire. Once on the roof the heat hit them. Nero, however, was just as excited as a child who has received a beautiful present. The scorching blaze, which made it almost impossible to remain on the flat roof, did not seem to bother him. While all of them took a step back, Nero went to the edge of the roof. "Beautiful, beautiful!" he called out with elation.

From their high position they watched the enormous sea of fire. The temple of Jupiter Stater was a red-hot inferno on the top of the hill, dominating the scene. The magnificent buildings at the Forum were in flames and the housing estates burnt fiercely. Every now and then, a fountain of sparks showered upward when a building collapsed. Heavy clouds of smoke drifted slowly over the surrounding land. In the dark of the evening the firelight would be seen many kilometres away from the city.

"Bring me a lyre," Nero ordered. His eyes shone feverishly as if reflecting the fire which he had lit.

Quickly the musical instrument was handed to the Emperor. He plucked the strings and tuned the lyre.

"How can the roaring of the flames best be put into words," he said musingly.

Nobody answered for fear of breaking the concentration of their lord and ruler, and thereby cause an attack of madness. If that occurred, their lives would not be safe any more.

Nero cleared his throat. "Bring me a mug of wine. This heat is making me thirsty . . . I say, Tigellinus, can't you temper that fire a bit?"

"I'll give orders to have this done immediately, oh divine Caesar," the man answered, knowing very well that this could never be done. It was impossible to make the Emperor understand this. But with this reply, the Emperor appeared satisfied.

"But make sure the fire won't go out, will you!?" Nero asked anxiously.

"I'll personally guarantee that it won't, Caesar."

Put at ease, Nero finished his wine. He tuned his instrument for a second time and started to sing. Again Nero used parts of Homerus' epic poem about the fire of Troy, inserting some of his own twisted and bombastic sentences. The song moved him. Tears were streaming down his cheeks, although this could also have been caused by the smoke.

At last the song was finished. The noblemen and senators made haste to praise him. Nero was as proud as a peacock.

"This time my song was perfect, wasn't it? Today I had an example of a burning city right in front of my eyes!"

All nodded like puppets, indicating in loud voices that it had been magnificent.

For a short while Nero continued to look at the fire. Then he left the roof, much to the relief of his retinue. He had sung his song and now the fire did not interest him anymore. In the large hall of the palace he gave a festive banquet in honour of the success of his song. The next day the company would return to Antium.

Everybody took part in the celebration, be it willingly or unwillingly. But, most of them did not participate whole-heartedly, preferring to leave and see if their possessions in the city had suffered in the fire. Others were certain that the fire had consumed their belongings. They had become as poor as a church-mouse. Nero, however, joyfully raised the mugs of wine. He was satisfied. The suffering of his people was of no concern to him.

During the meal Rufus, the chief of the bodyguard, approached Nero.

"The people are discontented, Caesar," he announced after having been granted permission to speak.

Nero reacted angrily. What a nuisance! Why could not an Emperor have a trouble-free party when he wanted to?

"What concern are the people to me?" he snarled.

Rufus felt very uneasy. In front of him was a tyrant who acted as his whims and fancies moved him, and he was aware that the people outside the palace were becoming rebellious. That this "mob" of people had to be reckoned with was beyond doubt. Therefore Rufus tried to convince Nero of the seriousness of the situation.

"The people are complaining because they do not have any shelter and they are forced to spend the night in the open."

"They are complaining? How unthankful! Is shelter of any significance when compared with the unsurpassable beauty of the song I made this evening?" Nero exclaimed dramatically, stretching out his arms.

The chief of the Pretorians realised that it was dangerous to oppose the Emperor but he lacked any other choice. He knew that he could count on the Pretorians; they would protect him in case of need. This gave him the courage to further interrupt Nero's drinking-bout.

"Oh divine Caesar, forgive me when I keep pressing the matter, but the situation is becoming worse by the hour. The people not only lack shelter but they also lack food. As you know, all supplies have been burnt. It's quite possible that the people will rebel!"

That gave Nero a fright.

"The people will rebel?" Seeking help, he looked at the noblemen and senators around him. Yet on none of their faces did he see a trace of pity. Their faces were like masks. Nervously, Nero plucked his red beard. Rebellion? That should be prevented at all cost!

"Just kill those rebels," he said.

"That means that I shall have to kill the whole population," Rufus answered.

Nero rose and paced up and down the hall. He did not know how to deal with this situation. Just like all other Roman Emperors, he loathed the common people. Yet he realised that the same people could become a danger if they rebelled against him. Besides, Nero was desperately in need of the people's favour when he, as charioteer or as singer, made his appearance in the arena or theatre. Who else would cheer him? Suddenly he had a solution for the problem.

"Immediately supply them with bread and wine," he ordered.

Yet, Rufus was not satisfied with this answer.

"But that is not going to put out the fire, oh divine Caesar," he said.

"Well, fight the fire and put it out then!" Nero screamed.

"Impossible!" reacted Seneca impulsively.

As if stung by a wasp, the Emperor turned around.

"I command it, and everything I command must be done!"

"But it is impossible to execute this command, oh Caesar," Seneca dared to answer back.

The tyrant's eyes narrowed.

"What? Do you openly admit that you are unable to execute my divine order?"

The men turned pale. If this did not work out, it could mean their death. Petronius tried to save the situation.

"Sometimes divine decrees are powerless," he said. "That happens when the decrees coming from the good gods, are directed to the evil gods of the underworld. Alas, that is the current situation. You, oh Caesar, in your incomprehensible wisdom, gave divine orders to put Rome on fire. You were lord and master over that fire. You lit it when you wanted to and you also could have it extinguished."

Nero nodded, flattered.

"But," Petronius continued, "due to your power, the fire has become so immense that even the gods of the underworld have come to look at it. They became jealous because only you could rule such an enormous fire. At the time that you were singing your beautiful song, they maliciously took possession of your fire. And that's why it can't be stopped at your command anymore, oh Caesar."

"Is that really true, Petronius? Did I make the gods of the underworld jealous?" Nero asked the question, moved to tears. "But then I must make a song about this. Bring me a lyre!"

Relieved, the courtiers breathed more freely. The danger had been averted, at least for the time being.

Suddenly Nero remembered the threatening rebellion again.

"How can we put out the fire? Shall we bring sacrifices?"

"On which altar do you suppose to do that, Caesar?" Rufus asked in a matter-of-fact voice. "The temple of Jupiter Stater has been reduced to ashes, the temple of Vesta is a blazing sea of fire and the altars of Isis have also been destroyed by the fire."

Nero became desperate. With large steps he paced up and down the hall and continuously plucked his beard.

"What else can we do?" he complained.

"The only solution is to deprive the fire of fuel by breaking down the houses that haven't been burnt as yet," Lucanus suggested.

"That's a good idea!" Nero cried out. "The people will then notice that I'm willing to do anything to please them. Tomorrow they will have bread and wine free of charge, and the fire will be stopped. What else could they want?"

Rufus took a deep breath. What he was going to say now could cost him his life, but he still counted on the help of the Pretorians.

"One more thing, oh divine Caesar. I have heard that the people say that you, Caesar, have started the fire, and they demand that the culprit should be punished!"

A deathly silence fell in the hall. Drops of sweat appeared on Nero's pale forehead. He breathed heavily. Suddenly his face brightened. A nasty laugh welled up in his throat.

"Tigellinus, you lit the fire, didn't you?"

"I only executed your order," he stammered.

"I know that, my dear Tigellinus. But I can never be punished for anything. I am a god, and gods are so inscrutably wise that the common mortals cannot judge if their deeds have been good or bad."

Nero was visibly relieved now that he had managed to wriggle out of this precarious situation.

But, Tigellinus felt far from comfortable. "But Caesar, are you saying that I should take your place?"

"Indeed, that's what I was saying," Nero said mockingly.

Tigellinus squirmed and tried desperately to save himself from this awful predicament.

"Oh Caesar, son of the gods, in your divine wisdom you know that I would willingly give my life for you, but . . ."

"Are you willing to do that?" Nero interrupted him. "That's all right, my dear friend. Carry on with it. I'm waiting." He settled himself comfortably in order not to miss anything of the spectacle. "Now, come on," he encouraged.

Tigellinus moistened his dry lips.

"But Caesar, who am I that by my death, I could reconcile the people with you," he called out desperately. "The people want a greater sacrifice."

"Indeed, Caesar," Seneca came to the unfortunate tribune's rescue. "Something has to be done that will divert the people's attention."

Nero sat up. New perspectives were opening up.

"That's a very bright idea, Seneca," he said. "But what should we do? . . . Oh, before I forget . . . Tigellinus, don't die just yet. We now have more important things to attend to."

Everybody was quiet, deep in thought. Seneca had given a good solution, but what had to be done next? Suddenly Tigellinus called out as if by inspiration, "The Christians!"

"But they are totally innocent." Seneca was terrified. He feared that this proposal would result in something different from what he would wish to see. He was kindly disposed toward the Christians. Thanks to his influence, the apostle Paul had been acquitted some time ago. But Nero beckoned with his hand.

"What about those Christians? Tell me!"

"Well, they are enemies of the country. They don't sacrifice to the gods, not even to you, oh Caesar. They drink the blood of young children, and they say their leader will become king over the whole earth. They also have a poor reputation with the people because of their witchcraft."

"That's enough! The Christians have lit the fire and they will have to pay for it," Nero cried out passionately.

"That means we have to plan this carefully, oh divine Caesar," coaxed Tigellinus. "The people should be influenced so that they themselves will demand the punishment of the Christians. At the same time the attention will be distracted from you."

Nero grinned. "Beautiful! I instruct you to prepare everything. But don't forget, it should be a spectacle never seen before and never to be seen again."

"The punishing of the Christians will be a great feast for all the people," Tigellinus promised.

He made his bow and left in a hurry. Ugh! He was cold with perspiration. It had certainly been a very anxious half an hour for him.

Some time later, he summoned some Jews to see him.

Seneca looked troubled. This had not been his intention. If the sadist Tigellinus and the tyrant Nero were making plans, then the future for the Christians looked very gloomy indeed!

# CHAPTER 9

## *THE "FEASTS" START*

The fire raged for six days and nights. When at last it was brought under control, ten of the fourteen districts which made up the inner city of Rome had been totally reduced to ashes.

Ancient Rome had become a glowing ash-heap. The reddish glare shone against the night-sky. Every now and then the flames blazed up briefly, their ghostly glimmer illuminating the burnt out ruins that were still standing.

Quintus could not help looking at it. Every evening he climbed the hill and stared in the distance. Over there, in that glow, were the charred bodies of his mother and Davus. He thought of them with an aching heart. Davus had been better off than his mother; at least he had been dead before the fire consumed his body. But his mother? She had probably been burnt alive.

With impotent rage against those who were responsible for the disaster, Quintus clenched his fists, his young heart crying out for vengeance. All of the eight hundred thousand homeless who had lost everything in the fire reacted in the same way. Many of them, like Quintus, mourned for relatives or friends.

Behind him he could hear the people in the tents that had been hurriedly pitched for them. A bit further along, men were hard at work building emergency dwellings by torchlight. During the day, Quintus had assisted them diligently. His knowledge of tent-making came in very handy. While he was working he did not think of his sorrow and thirst for revenge, but at night the memories flashed through his mind again. Then he recalled the many discussions that he had with the old coppersmith, and how he had always made sure that his mother was alright before he went to bed.

He was startled, when he suddenly noticed a man standing next to him.

"We've had the worst," the man said, nodding his head in the direction of the city.

Uninterested, Quintus shrugged his shoulders. What did it matter. As far as he was concerned the rest of Rome could burn down as well!

"And to think that the fire was started deliberately," the man said again.

"Yes, I know. Nero lit it."

"Nero? What makes you think that? That is what the real culprits want us to believe but it's not what happened."

Taken by surprise, Quintus looked at the man. This was something new he was hearing.

"Who did it then?" he asked with renewed interest.

If it were sure that Nero was not to blame, perhaps the real villains would come within the reach of his revenge.

The man pulled Quintus toward him by his tunic.

"The Christians," he whispered.

Dismayed, the boy stared at the speaker. "The Christians?" he repeated in disbelief.

"As sure as I'm standing here. During one of their religious feasts they became hysterical and set fire to all the houses in the neighbourhood. The old and corrupt Rome had to disappear, they said, and anyone who tried to put out the fire was killed by them."

"Nonsense," Quintus said fiercely. "To my knowledge they didn't have a religious feast on that day, and besides that, I've spoken to people who saw soldiers of Nero throwing burning torches into houses."

Cunningly, the man closed his eyes.

"What does that prove?" he asked. "Nothing, I tell you! There are also many Christians among the soldiers. They had been converted by a man named Paul, whom they were guarding some years ago. The Christians made good use of this situation. They let the soldiers set fire to the houses so that they could lay the blame on Emperor Nero."

The man looked at Quintus triumphantly, as if to say, "Well, what do you say to that?"

Quintus shook his head. He just could not believe that Aquila and Priscilla, Demas, and the many other Christians with whom he had become acquainted during the past months, were capable of deliberately causing such a terrible disaster. Satan, however, was lying in wait. Since the time of Paradise, he had become an expert in deceiving people and he exploited the present situation as much as possible.

Suddenly, Quintus remembered the words of old Davus, "Do you know that the Christians believe that their world will be consumed by fire? Well to prove that their words are true, they themselves have to kindle that fire." Unintentionally, he had repeated the words out aloud.

"See! You are saying it yourself!" the man called out exultantly.

Quintus was at his wit's end. His doubts grew by the minute. He did not even notice that the stranger had gone away, and had entered into conversation with somebody else a bit further along. The devil smiled, satisfied with the result. The poison had started to work. Rome's fire had stopped raging but in the hearts of the people a new fire was being kindled; a fire that would be even more terrible and devastating than the fire that had consumed Rome.

The next morning Quintus heard several people exclaiming: "The Christians to the lions!" Every hour the outcry became stronger and it swelled into a mighty chant which could be heard over the Campagna where many had found shelter. It echoed over the burnt ruins and penetrated into Nero's palace. The emperor smiled. Tigellinus had done a good job. He was still doing everything he could to stir up the people's fury. "The Christians to the lions!" This became the demand by tormented people who wanted to revenge the loss of relatives and possessions.

The deceitful lie about the Christians was readily believed. This was because the people did not understand the Christians, and they could now aim their revenge at something that was within their reach. Compensation was demanded for all the misery the people had suffered. "The Christians to the lions!" Quintus, too, was infected by the general overpowering mood and shouted as loudly as all the others. Ah, now somebody would pay for the pain his mother had suffered, for the agony she had to endure, and for the grief that had befallen him. Yes, that is how it should be: the Christians to the lions!

Quintus, too, gathered in the crowd when the soldiers came to arrest the believers. This was easy for them to do because most of the time the Christians had formed themselves into separate groups and the people were only too willing to point them out to the soldiers.

"There, Centurion. In that tent there are a few more."

Praying and encouraging each other, the victims readily let themselves be carried along. The crowd snorted with contempt. Ugh, what cowards they were! They wondered how the Christians would behave in the arena. Would it be worthwhile to go and have a look when they were torn to pieces by the ferocious animals?

In the mean time, the people's attention was diverted as a cart carrying food arrived in the camp. Everybody flocked toward it. Hands stretched out greedily to grab the free bread and wine. But the cart was well guarded. This was necessary because previously the crowd had stormed the cart and the contents had been torn to pieces and trampled upon. Then nobody had received anything. The soldiers accompanying the transport, had gained a lot of experience since the fire. With drawn swords they formed a ring around the cart, leaving an opening just wide enough for one man to pass through. The rudest of the crowd had already experienced how sharp the swords were. The distribution was now far more efficient. Those who wanted to push were warned by others to stay calm. There was enough for everyone, wasn't there? And when the cart was empty, another would soon arrive. In Nero's empire there was no need to be hungry. Long live Caesar!

Quintus waited patiently for his turn. He only had to look after himself, so why make a fuss?

That evening Quintus was among the crowds of people who flocked to the gardens of the imperial palace.

After the fire, Nero had done everything to make a favourable impression on the people and had even opened his gardens to the public.

Yet, this evening there was a special reason to visit them. The emperor had promised the people a grand party to celebrate the beginning of the rebuilding of Rome. The feast would last for some weeks and the main performers would be Christians. Tonight was the opening night. Chariot races were to be held in the Imperial Gardens, in which Nero also would participate. An unlimited amount of wine from the palace-cellars would be served free of charge. A special attraction would be the festive lighting. According to the announcements, this would be more fantastic than had ever been seen before.

Many people tried to guess what this lighting would be. But nobody could predict the satanic plan which had sprung from Nero's mind.

As anxious as everyone else, Quintus shuffled with the crowd through the garden gate. It was not totally dark yet, but he did not want to arrive too late. It would be a pity to miss the races or the lighting. He tried to catch a glimpse of what was coming. Between the trees and shrubs he saw numerous poles with torches tied to them. These would presently be set on fire.

Momentarily he felt disappointed. Was this the extraordinary lighting? Or was there something special about those torches? Hurriedly, he forced his way through the crowd to investigate. In the gardens there was much shouting and singing, loud enough to raise the dead. Many had already profited from the freely-served wine and were drunk even before the feast had started.

Quintus had reached the nearest torch. An incredulous look came into his eyes when saw what it was . . . a human being! A living person had been tied to the pole and wound in pieces of cloth like a mummy so that only the face could be seen. The clothes had been drenched in sulphur, pitch, and resin. That was Nero's festive lighting. Living people! . . .

There were many of these torches in the garden, perhaps even hundreds of them. Fire-pots had been placed between the poles. The slaves would soon throw perfumes into these pots to drive away the stench of burning sulphur, pitch, and human flesh.

"They are all Christians," somebody friendly informed Quintus.

For a moment, enormous pity for these wretched people welled up in Quintus, but then his thirst for revenge got the better of him.

"Serves them right!" he answered. "My mother was burnt alive and now they themselves can feel what it was like."

"You are right," the other admitted.

Quintus wandered from torch to torch and looked at them attentively. He saw the faces of men and women, old people as well as young ones. Boys and girls, and even very small children, were among them. The crowd, many of them drunk, enjoyed themselves tremendously and made faces at the mummies. A young woman with brown eyes looked down at Quintus so intensely that he had to avert his gaze. Quickly he walked on. But those eyes seemed to follow him and took away the pleasure he had felt in anticipating the suffering of the Christians. Maybe Christ Himself had looked down from the cross in the same manner, he suddenly thought. Yes, perhaps exactly in the same way, without a trace of fear or revenge. Had not Jesus Christ prayed, "Father, forgive them, for they do not know what they are doing"?

So what! Christ! Quintus shook off that thought. It was just nonsense. Look at those torches! When things became bad, Christ was just as powerless as all the other gods. Why didn't He rescue His followers from these poles of torture? No, He could not even save Himself from the cross! Just compare Him with the Roman gods! They had sometimes taken revenge on their opponents in a terrible manner. But Christ? No! And then they say that this God is a God of love. Strange love, to have your followers tortured like this!

Quintus walked on. He stopped near a pole to which a boy had been tied. This boy had his eyes closed but his face shone and a faint smile was on his lips.

"That will change when the flames tickle him," someone mocked.

"He's praying," Quintus said softly.

The bystanders laughed loudly.

Quintus turned abruptly and walked away. Suddenly he loathed the drunken nonsense around him.

Unintentionally, he again found himself near the young woman with the brown eyes. This time he fled. He could not stand her gaze any longer. "Christ Himself is looking at you," it flashed through his mind. "Just as Jesus used the tongues of Paul, Peter, and many others to speak to his people, He now uses the eyes of that woman to look at you."

But Quintus did not want this thought to bother him. He felt relieved when the sound of trumpets announced the arrival of Nero. Good! The feast was to start and would bring some amusement. Together with the drunken crowd he took up his position along the track where the chariot-races were to be held. All eyes turned to the gate that gave access to the palace.

Several slaves commenced lighting the human torches. Then the gate opened and Nero appeared, preceded by his charioteers and surrounded by courtiers. He stood in his chariot which was inlaid with gold and ivory, and drawn by four white horses. Nero himself was clothed in a purple mantle, with the crown of victory already on his head. Escorted by a cohort of Pretorians, the procession made a tour through the gardens.

The public cheered enthusiastically. "Hail to Caesar! Hail to Caesar!" The shouting drowned out the groans of the burning Christians. The horses were skittish; it seemed as if they sensed something was odd about the burning torches. Yet, the people cheered the instigator of this terrible evil. "Hail to Caesar!"

Quintus overheard part of a conversation behind him.

"Those Christians can only blame themselves. They were given a choice. Either, die a martyr or bring an offering to the emperor and renounce their God. Then they would be set free. Only a few took advantage of this opportunity. Most of those stupid fanatics chose martyrdom instead."

Quintus looked around to see who was speaking but he could not find the speaker. Still, the words stuck in his mind. Slowly he began to realise that the God of the Christians had to be someone very special indeed. He could not think of any Roman god or goddess for whom he would be willing to offer his life. He tried to imagine what it meant to be faced with a choice like the Christians had. Suddenly he realised that the people who were now dying on the poles of torture had been extraordinarily brave when they had chosen to die. Yes, they had shown a courage that was supernatural.

This thought haunted him. But then Christ Himself had not acted cowardly either, as Quintus had first thought. He had possessed the power to sweep away all His adversaries off the surface of the earth. He had surrendered of His own free will to suffer and die. Had His love for His people then been so great? The God of the Christians was the God of love after all!

Yet, Quintus could not explain why Christ did not free His followers from all those torments. He began to realise that the suffering of Christ had been even greater than that of these people. They knew that they were morally supported by the prayers of their fellow-Christians, and they also had a direct contact with their God in heaven. Jesus had been forsaken not only by men but above all by God.

Quintus became somewhat uneasy because of these thoughts. He forced his way to the front of the spectators to watch Nero now that he had finished his tour. The races would start soon and perhaps this would distract his mind. He stood in the front-row when the drivers put their chariots in position. He saw the smiling face of Nero.

"Why doesn't God strike down that tyrant with lightning?" Quintus thought. And a moment later, "Would the Christians, after these terrible things, still love Nero? If so, then their faith must give them tremendous strength."

All was ready for the contest. But it would not really be a contest seeing that Nero was one of the competitors. Everybody knew beforehand that he would be the winner, because no charioteer would dare challenge Nero and cross the finish line in front of him. It would cost him his life if he did. Despite this, the people roared with enthusiasm. The suffering and dying Christians behind them were already forgotten, and the initial excitement of the lighting spectacle had waned. Occasionally somebody coughed because of the irritating smoke that slowly drifted over the gardens.

Quintus walked with the crowd to the opposite side of the race-course to watch the finish. As he passed one of the torches, he could not help looking up at it.

Through the smoke and flames he looked straight into the brown eyes of the young woman. She looked at him intently and Quintus thought he saw a smile in her eyes. Was she still smiling while in such pain? That was indeed extraordinary.

Slowly, Quintus stepped backward but he could not break away from her gaze. Fear overwhelmed him and he ran away. Suddenly, a sentence from Aquila's sermon flashed through his mind: "Whatever you did for the least of these brothers of Mine, you did for me." Yes, and that did not only refer to the good works done to Christians but also the bad ones, of course. In fact, here, in Nero's garden, Christ was burnt to death! Quintus became more and more troubled.

"But I didn't take part in it, did I?" he muttered.

"Yes, you did," his conscience accused him, "even though you yourself didn't set the torches alight. The whole of the Roman nation is guilty because it didn't protest against Nero's plan."

Quintus could not bear to be in the garden any longer. He wanted to leave. Behind him he heard cheering. Nero is crossing the finish-line as victor, he thought, but it did not interest him. The suffocating smoke of sulphur and pitch, mixed with the abominable stench of burning human flesh, oppressed him.

"Oh God, if I too, am guilty of this terrible drama, will there still be forgiveness for me?" he sobbed.

In this distressed state, Quintus left the Imperial Gardens. Aimlessly he wandered among the ruins of ancient Rome. Here and there the heat could still be felt.

Abruptly, he changed course. He had become very uneasy about fires.

# CHAPTER 10

## *IN THE CATACOMBS*

Between the still smouldering ruins at the Forum, Quintus met Demas and Caecillia. This further confused him, for since he had left to go to Hermes' place, Quintus had not been back to the tent factory. Nor had he bothered to inquire about the well-being of Aquila and the others. The fire, and the death of his mother and Davus had, as it were, cut the bonds with the past. Anything that reminded him of his old life he had unconsciously put out his mind. Moreover, he had gone along with the general hatred toward the Christians, making him quite unsympathetic toward their plight. It was therefore, understandable that Quintus was confused when he saw Demas and his girlfriend.

"Are you still alive?" Demas asked in astonishment. "We really thought you had perished in the fire."

When Quintus did not answer, he continued, "Sestianus told us that you had returned to the city. Afterward we inquired everywhere and finally we found some people who had seen you run blindly into a burning street. They told us that you were looking for your mother."

"My mother was burnt to death," Quintus said hoarsely.

Demas and Caecillia were touched by Quintus' sorrow. They understood the great grief that was expressed in those few words. Demas did not know what to say. He put his arm around his friend's shoulders and Caecillia tenderly took his hand.

"I'll pray to God to comfort you," she said warmly.

Quintus shook his head. "It's no use. I've prayed to God and asked Him to save my mother but He doesn't want anything to do with me," he answered softly.

"That's not true, Quintus," Caecillia answered. "I don't know why God didn't save your mother, but there is one thing I'm certain of: He is concerned about you. God is in control of everybody's lives."

Quintus, however, kept shaking his head.

"You don't know all that I've done. And you also don't know what is happening there." He pointed in the direction of the palace-gardens. The distant shouting and singing still rang in their ears.

In a few words he explained what he had seen. "And I too, am guilty of that," he cried out.

Demas looked aghast and Caecillia could not suppress a cry of horror. "It's not true, is it?" she stammered.

"But you don't have to lay the blame for this on yourself," Demas said to Quintus, when he had found his voice.

"Yes, indeed, I do," Quintus persisted. "All of us who were in the gardens before the feast started, are guilty. We should have protested before the torches were lit. We should have demanded that the Christians be taken off those poles of torture before it was too late. But we laughed about it. Yes, I too! And that's why I also am responsible for it."

He started to sob again. Demas and Caecillia did not know how to handle the situation. Desperately, they searched for words of comfort. "When you ask God, He will certainly forgive you," Demas said at last. "Even the murderer on the cross was accepted by Christ. Just imagine, a murderer!"

It seemed as if Demas' words did not penetrate. Absent-mindedly, Quintus looked off into the darkness.

"We'd better take him with us to the meeting so that Sestianus can have a talk with him," Caecillia suggested.

Despite his distress, Quintus looked up. "Do you still have your meetings?" he asked in surprise. "In these circumstances, when lots of Christians are being captured and subjected to all kinds of torture?"

Demas nodded. "If ever there was a reason to meet, it's now. We need each other's prayers and support more than ever before, and above all, the communion with God."

Quintus could not understand this.

"But in this way you make it very easy for the soldiers," he said. "They will just raid a meeting and capture more than a hundred people at once. I believe that you are acting irresponsibly."

His concern for his friends had made him forget his grief.

Demas set Quintus' mind at ease. "We don't let ourselves be caught as easily as on the first day. We realise that such an attitude doesn't serve any purpose. When we meet now, we take all precautions. Our meetings are even more secret than before, and they are usually held in the old quarries just outside the city. You'll remember that these quarries consist of a maze of passages from which the stone has been mined. If the quarries were to be raided unexpectedly, they'll never find us."

While talking they started on their way. Quintus walked with them. Deep down, he longed to talk to Sestianus about all the things that were worrying him. He looked with envy at his friends. They did not seem to have any difficulty in completely yielding themselves to God's leadership, and they were convinced that their sins were forgiven. At the same time they had enough courage to confess that they loved Christ, even though it could mean their death if they were caught. But suddenly he realised that he also could be arrested if he was present at their meeting. For a moment he hesitated, but the desire to relieve his feelings, and to hear more about that God for whom the Christians were willing to die, even as martyrs, made him continue. Besides, there was always the chance to be freed, he reassured himself. He could always curse God, bring an offering to the emperor, and nothing would happen to him. Encouraged by this thought, he walked on.

Demas, meanwhile, related what had happened to him during and after the fire. He told Quintus that the tent factory had been saved and none of the staff had been imprisoned as yet. Quintus only heard half of what his friend was telling him. He was too busy thinking about his own problems.

They had now left the city and were trying to find the path that led to the quarries. This was rather difficult in the dark. Yet Demas had not taken a lamp with him for fear of being betrayed by its glow.

"It must be here," he said, walking up a narrow path that wound between shrubs and boulders. In single file they walked on. First Demas, then Caecillia and last of all Quintus. Suddenly they stopped in fright. A man had jumped onto the path directly in front of them.

"Where are you going?" he asked.

"Peace be to you," Demas answered after he had recovered from his fright.

"Who are you?"

"I'm Demas, and with me are Caecillia and Quintus. We are on our way to the meeting with Sestianus."

"Password?"

"*Sursum Corda* (lift up your hearts)."

"Peace be to you," the man replied. "Just follow this path to the cross-road. Turn to the right when you reach the white stone."

They said goodbye and continued on their way. With these directions they could follow the path without any trouble despite the darkness. They were stopped twice more before they had reached the entrance to the quarries. There, another watchman was waiting. He led them into the cave where they met some fellow-Christians.

"Just wait here for a moment," the man commanded, and walked away. Silently, they grouped together in the darkness. In the distance they saw the faint light of the entrance. For the rest it was pitch-dark around them. Only the breathing and the occasional shuffling of feet indicated that several people were in the cave. From time to time the watchman brought in more visitors.

"How many are there now?" somebody asked.

"Fifteen," the watchman answered.

"Then I'll escort these people further."

A lamp was lit in the corner of the cave.

"Just follow me," said the man who carried the lamp.

In single file they walked along the passage. The person at the rear hardly profited from the light of the lamp. The guide appeared to be a stone-cutter because he knew his way through the maze of passages very well. Confidently he led the group of Christians to their destination.

"Don't you think that we'll be safe here?" Demas said softly to Quintus. "Anybody who doesn't know the place will never be able find us."

Quintus grumbled something. He was in no mood for talking. For that matter, nobody said anything.

The gloomy atmosphere of the passages had an oppressing effect on the group. Moreover, the light of the lamp threw freakish shadows on the uneven rock-faces, giving the place a ghostly appearance. Consequently most were glad when a faint murmur of voices could be heard in the distance. Sooner than expected, they found themselves standing in a room. It was lit by oil-lamps and some torches that were hanging on the wall. A rough wooden table, which had been placed against a wall, was the only piece of furniture in the room. About thirty people were sitting on the ground in small groups, talking to one another. Most of them, however, were absorbed in prayer. Those who had just arrived, blinked their eyes because of the bright light.

"There's Quintus!" some people called out, very surprised to see him.

He was soon surrounded by people who he knew from the meetings at Aquila's. The Jew and his wife were not present but Sestianus was. With tears of joy, he greeted Quintus, whom he had thought to be dead.

Naturally, everyone wanted to know where Quintus had been. The Christians knew that after the fire he had disappeared without a trace. But Demas understood that his friend was not in the mood for talking.

"Brothers and sisters," he said, "don't bother Quintus, please. He appreciates your concern but he is too shocked by what has happened to him. Perhaps a talk with Sestianus will help him."

The presbyter understood and took Quintus away to speak to him privately.

Demas then told the people what he had heard about the events in the Imperial Gardens. Appalled, and with increasing horror, they listened. Naturally, none of the Christians had gone to the feasts, and so this was the first they had heard of the events that had taken place there.

"It can't be true!" someone muttered.

With this terrible news, an oppressive silence settled on those in the cave. When the guide brought in another group, they were also informed of the events in Rome.

"But this calls for revenge. We can't tolerate all this, can we?" one of the men called out.

"Don't talk like that, Brother," the answer was. "It's written: 'Vengeance is Mine.' And that is good. Only God is mighty enough to punish the instigators and authors of this evil. Punishment from human beings, however severe, would be lacking in many respects. Honestly, leave it to God and don't sin because of your thirst for revenge. Remember what is written: 'to him who strikes you on the right cheek, offer the left one also!' "

The first speaker bowed his head. "I just cannot understand it," he said.

A murmur rose from the group. Many of them could not understand why God asked this abominable suffering of the Christians. (Even now, nineteen centuries later, we still cannot understand why God deemed this necessary to increase His church.)

"Let us pray," a woman said in a trembling voice.

Silently they, all knelt down.

Meanwhile Quintus had been talking with Sestianus. He was comforted by the encouraging words of the presbyter. These words were totally different from those he had heard during the past few days, when he had heard nothing else but cries for revenge. Then the god of vengeance had still been sitting high on his throne.

Sestianus, however, talked about love and mercy. The desire to belong to Christ and to serve Him, was slowly beginning to grow in Quintus. This desire became stronger as the discussion continued, despite a voice in his heart which warned him that it was sheer madness to become a Christian during these times. It was like playing with one's life. Yet it was precisely this danger that made it decisive for him. This God must be different from the Roman and Greek gods! Yes, it must be true that this God was the only, true God, even though His ways were incomprehensible.

"Can I . . . will I be allowed to be baptised?" he asked at last.

Sestianus answered in the affirmative. They discussed matters a little more and then returned to the cavern. Everyone was kneeling on the ground, praying. Silently, Quintus and Sestianus knelt down with the congregation. When they had finished, the presbyter signalled that it was time to start the service.

The service commenced in a similar fashion to those that Quintus had experienced often at Aquila's. They sang and prayed after which one of the brothers taught the congregation some new songs that highlighted their present situation.

Sestianus then read Mark 13:9-13:

*But take heed to yourselves; for they will deliver you up to councils; and you will be beaten in synagogues; and you will stand before governors and kings for My sake, to bear testimony before them. And the Gospel must be preached to all nations. And when they bring you to trial and deliver you up, do not be anxious be-*

*forehand what you are to say, for it is not you who speak but the Holy Spirit. And brother will deliver up brother to death, and the father his child, and children will rise against parents and have them put to death.*

The focus for his sermon was the thirteenth verse.

*And you will be hated by all for My Name's sake. But he who endures to the end will be saved.*

"Christ Himself has foretold," the presbyter proclaimed, "that we will be hated and must suffer for His Name. Not because the people want to do this to us, but because God wills it. And why do we have to suffer so much? To this question also, Christ Himself gives us the answer, 'to bear testimony before governors and kings.' Our suffering, therefore, is intended to increase God's church. Christ has suffered immeasurably for our sake. Should we then not be willing to suffer for Him just a little?" the preacher called out.

The congregation listened breathlessly.

"But don't fear," he continued, "Christ did not only promise us that in the darkest hour He will be with us but also that all who persevere till the end will be saved. And isn't this a wonderful rich promise? We shouldn't seek the power to persevere in ourselves but, by praying without ceasing, ask our Father in heaven for it."

It was deathly quiet in the cave. Everyone was absorbed in the preaching. It was no longer Sestianus, but Christ Himself who was speaking to the congregation through Sestianus. "At this moment God is busy separating the chaff from the wheat," Sestianus continued. "With the winnow in His hand, He is treading the threshing-floor and only that which is pure and precious, will be left. But, remember that, when bread is baked from the grain, it must not only be threshed but also ground and crushed. Grain which is not ground, is used again for sowing a new crop. For what service God has destined us, I do not know. We can either be sown or ground. Whatever happens, it will be to the glory of God's Name."

Sestianus concluded his sermon with words of comfort and encouragement.

It was now time for the baptism of Quintus. Sestianus began by saying that he was very glad that Quintus wanted to be baptised. He pointed out that Quintus had the courage to follow Christ despite the difficult and dangerous times. Having read a baptismal form, Sestianus asked Quintus to kneel. There was no baptismal font so the presbyter used a stone bottle. From this he poured water over Quintus' head three times while pronouncing the well-known words: "I baptise you in the Name of the Father, and of the Son, and of the Holy Spirit."

"Amen," the congregation responded.

After the baptism, they thanked God in prayer. Then everyone stepped forward to welcome the new member with a kiss, as was the custom among the Christians in those days. The baptismal ceremony was finished. Somebody gave Sestianus some bread and wine and he gave thanks to the Lord.

"Amen," the congregation said again.

The deacons dealt out the bread and the wine to everyone who was present. With this celebration of the Lord's Supper, the service in the catacomb had finished. Sestianus thanked the Lord again and once more the congregation answered with "Amen."

Sestianus persuaded Quintus to go with him to Hermes' house, and while waiting for the guide to lead them to the exit, they talked to Demas and Caecillia. After having brought one group away, he returned with the alarming news that soldiers were patrolling the Via Appia. It had become known to them that the Christians were having a meeting. The soldiers restricted themselves to guarding the road by which the Christians had to go home because they realised that searching the quarries' maze of passages would be a waste of time.

The message brought some tension in the cave. Sestianus proposed that they remain in the cave for a while. Perhaps the soldiers would withdraw again.

But the situation became more serious when, after an hour, the road still was not safe. Especially the slaves who served non-Christian masters, became worried. Would they still be in time for work? They found themselves caught between two fires. If they left in very small groups or alone, they might not be seen. Still, if they waited any longer it would become too light and practically impossible to leave the quarries unobserved.

They did as planned. The bravest ones left first to try to deceive the soldiers. The others waited anxiously.

After some time the guide returned. "It seems rather easy," he said. "They have left in small groups and we arranged that they would imitate the call of a night-bird when they had got away safely. From each of the three groups we heard the signal."

Everyone was relieved. The men and women had safely left the cave but more importantly there was now a reasonable chance for all to get away. A few of them, who had nothing to do during the day, preferred to stay quietly in the cave.

"You can stay here, too," Sestianus said to Quintus.

The latter shook his head firmly. "I'm not afraid," he said. Yet, he felt strangely tense when they set out.

"May God protect you," the guide said to them.

"Amen," Sestianus replied.

Cautiously, they walked down the winding path that led to the main road. Quintus admired Caecillia who walked bravely along with them. He thought she had a lot of courage. She knew very well that the walk was not without danger. Friends had urged her to remain in the cave but she did not want to leave Demas.

The four of them had reached the road. Sestianus, who walked in front, signalled with his hand for them to stop.

Quietly, the little group squatted down between the shrubs, alert for danger. After some time, a few soldiers walked past slowly. When the sound of their steps had died down, the presbyter stood up.

"It's safe now, I think," he whispered.

With a few steps they reached the road.

Unfortunately for them, the previous group had been somewhat careless. One of the soldiers was surprised when he saw a few people step out of the bushes close to him. While he remained motionless he saw another person. These must be the Christians, he thought. Quickly he warned his centurion. The centurion promptly placed his cohort in position. The other soldiers kept to their normal patrol. A grin of satisfaction swept over the centurion's face when he saw Sestianus and his companions stepping out onto the road. Silently, the four of them were arrested. They did not even have a chance to utter a cry of warning. Roughly the soldiers dragged them further into the field where they were thrown into a pit and closely guarded. More Christians were taken prisoner in the same manner, because from time to time new victims were brought in.

Quintus counted at least twenty people. They were all ordered to stand up, bound together with ropes and, guarded by several soldiers, they were marched off in the direction of the city.

# CHAPTER 11

## *IN THE ARENA*

Quintus did not offer any resistance while he let himself be led. It seemed as if a thick fog was hanging in his head. What he had experienced during the past week had been too much. Firstly, the all-consuming fire had swept away sweet memories of a happy and pleasant past. Ancient Rome with its familiar nooks and crannies did not exist any more. It had become a desolate ruin in which fires still blazed spasmodically. The city of Rome was to be rebuilt by Nero and the reconstruction had already started. It would be a strange Rome; a city without the old coppersmith and without his mother. Quintus suppressed the inclination to think about the past. The memories of recent days demanded his attention: the drunk people in Nero's gardens, and the Christians at the poles of torture.

"A similar fate is awaiting you also." The thought flashed through his mind. "For you too are a Christian." It was the first time since his arrest that this thought entered his mind. He became very afraid. Would he have enough faith to endure these tortures? Of course, he could always sacrifice to the Emperor and curse God. Then he would be free again.

This idea comforted him somewhat. Stealthily, he looked about him. He did not know the man next to him. Caecillia and another girl, walked in front of him, erect and brave. She did not react to the rude jokes the soldiers made.

"That girl doesn't seem to have any fear at all," Quintus thought, and to be honest, he felt ashamed. Caecillia would never know that Quintus was lifted from his despair by her attitude. He asked God to give him the same faith and courage as Caecillia had. At the same time he realised that this was the first time since leaving the cave, that he was thinking about God again. It frustrated him. Was he such a bad Christian?

At the same time the devil saw his opportunity. "Yes, you have been a Christian for too short a time to die for your faith already. Just bring an offering to the Emperor; nobody will blame you for that. You are still so young!"

Quintus tried to rid himself of these thoughts. Again he looked at Caecillia. She was young too. In a few months time she was to marry Demas, but she certainly would not deny her God. Quintus did not know how to figure it all out. Sestianus was walking behind him and he wished he could talk it over with him. He shortened his step.

"Is a Christian allowed to flee?" he whispered, turning his head.

"For sure," was the whispered reply. "And if you still have a task in this world, God will surely let you succeed."

"Quiet there!" a soldier snarled. A whip-lash added force to his words.

Quintus felt a biting pain in his cheek but he had something else to concentrate his thoughts on.

Flee!

He gave his handcuffs a tug. These had been fastened faultlessly and expertly. After some effort he had a pair of raw wrists while the handcuffs had not even opened a millimetre. Discouraged, he stopped trying, and wearily continued his walk with the small group.

In the time of the Emperors, Rome did not have many prisons. To a certain extent, the Roman citizenship protected the people against imprisonment.

Remember what happened to Paul and Silas in the prison of Philippi. Paul said there, "They beat us publicly without a trial, even though we are Roman citizens, and threw us into prison." In those days, criminals were sent to the galleys, to the School for Gladiators, or punished by decapitation.

The few prisons that had not been destroyed by the fire, were filled to capacity with Christians. Quintus and the rest of the group of prisoners were dragged from one prison to the next. But everywhere they meet the same remark: no more room!

The soldiers became tired and moody because of the traipsing around and treated the Christians roughly and indifferently. The group halted in front of Nero's palace. The centurion went inside to ask the Prefectus Pretorio to inquire where to bring the prisoners. To free them, because there was no room, would be too ridiculous. After about ten minutes he returned.

"Just bring them to the imperial arena," he ordered, visibly relieved that he would get rid of the group.

"Well, you are greatly honoured," one of the soldiers grinned. "The last ones to be arrested and still chosen to open the games in a few hours time!"

The prisoners shuddered with horror. Would they really have such a short time to prepare themselves for their martyrdom?

Quintus looked at Caecillia again. The girl was still walking erect and courageously, and did not show any trace of tiredness or emotion. A young man at the front of the group saw matters differently. He let himself fall prostrate to the ground and shouted that he did not want to go to the arena. He cursed God and implored to be allowed to bring an offering to the Emperor. Immediately the centurion gave orders to free him and bring him to the Prefectus Urbanus — the Chief Justice.

"Are there any more who have changed their minds?" the centurion called out loudly.

Quintus hesitated and his eyes followed the man who was being led away. Should he? At that moment Caecillia turned and looked him straight in the eyes. Did the girl feel what was going on in his mind? Suddenly he had to think of the brown eyes of the woman on the torture-pole. He drew a deep breath and did not move his gaze from straight ahead as the centurion walked along the rows of prisoners and repeated his question.

"Quick! March!" the centurion ordered.

The procession began to move again and Quintus felt wonderfully relieved. The first rays of the sun shone on the walls of the Imperial Palace as the prisoners entered the arena.

Amid tripping and stumbling, the Christians ended in the underground dungeons. It was musty and humid. The cells were slightly wet and a thin layer of rotten straw lay on the floor.

The wild animals were locked up right next to the dungeons. They became uneasy when they scented human flesh. Restlessly, they walked up and down. Every now and then the underground vault was shaken by the mighty roars from the lions. The beasts had not eaten anything for four days and they were mad with hunger. They had been purposely teased and aroused by a hunk of meat that was placed in front of the cages, just out of their reach. The wild dogs whined in fear when the lions and tigers raised their voices. This changed into a penetrating bark when they became aware of the Christians.

A terrible fear seized Quintus and he nearly stopped breathing. He was afraid. Yes, even more than afraid! He broke out into a cold sweat. He felt sick. He wanted to leave, leave this horrible cave. Yet, flight was impossible. These dungeons had only one exit and that exit led to the arena. The boy thought that he would be driven crazy with fear. Only now he understood the words of the psalmist: "The cords of death held me in deep despair; the terrors of the grave caused me to languish."

Indeed, there was no comfort for these pangs of death; no word of encouragement could bring any relief. Here man had to cope alone. All by himself? No! Only Christ had been the One who had to undergo this fear all by Himself, but now He stands by His children in the hour of agony.

"Let us pray," Quintus heard as if from afar the voice of Sestianus.

Automatically, he knelt with the others on the dirty floor. The first part of the prayer passed him by, but then he heard a few words that struck him. He concentrated again and prayed with them. He felt his fear gradually disappearing. A beneficial pleasant calm came over him. The words, "A peace beyond all understanding," now had a clear message for him.

After the prayer Quintus stood up and joined Demas who was sitting on the floor with Caecillia. They did not speak to each other, so as not to disturb the sacred atmosphere that pervaded the dungeon after the prayer. Together, they listened when somebody said an encouraging word or recited part of Scripture. The roaring of the wild animals did not matter any more. They could only harm the body. The Christians knew that their souls were safe.

Suddenly the grille was opened and another stream of people was pushed inside. The dungeon was now filled to capacity. Even the guards asked themselves if it really was the intention to kill all those people on the same day. That, indeed, was the intention of Nero. The "feast" would be spectacular with many "contributors."

Stepping over legs and bodies, Sestianus went over to the young people. "I think it will be particularly difficult for you," he said, putting his hand upon Quintus' head. "You have been a Christian for only a few hours and God is calling you already. Are you prepared for that?"

"Yes, I know where I'm going," Quintus answered.

"I prayed to God to strengthen you in particular, my boy."

Then he turned to Demas and Caecillia.

"Are you willing to accept you won't be united in marriage here on earth? But afterward — perhaps already in a few hours time — you will go together to the heavenly marriage hall. You will be guests of honour at the wedding-feast of the Lamb and you will be crowned with the crown of martyrdom."

"What are they going to do with us, Sestianus?" Demas asked.

"Only God knows . . . and the devil. But humanly speaking, it won't be pleasant. One thing I know for sure: with our death we will glorify God. Pray God that He will be gracious to you in the hour of death, and remember: our suffering will be of short duration. It will be over in a quarter of an hour at the most. After that, eternal blissful life awaits us. Maybe Christ will soften our pain, or maybe He will take us to Himself very quickly. Our greatest comfort is that people can kill our body but our souls belong to our Saviour Jesus Christ, both in life and in death."

"I'm not afraid for myself," Quintus answered, "but if all believers are killed, nothing will be left of God's church in Rome. She will be totally exterminated."

The presbyter smiled.

"Don't worry about that, Quintus. God would never permit this if the coming of His kingdom was harmed by it. Remember the apostle Paul. He was imprisoned here in Rome for two years. Many thought: what can a prisoner do for God's church? But look what he was able to do! Even the soldiers who guarded him, were influenced by his preaching. Now that they have taken to the field again with their legions, they bring the Gospel, although unintentionally, to the furthest borders of the Roman Empire. And what do you think of the things that have happened the last few days, and are still happening? Soon the whole world will know that Rome had been burnt and the Christians have been tortured. As a result, the name of Christ, and the names of the Christians, will be on many lips. Really, the position of God's church is not as bad as you might think it is. But one question I cannot answer: why God, who is Almighty, is choosing this way. We'd better trust that it is good what He is doing."

Sestianus stood up and walked away. Quintus' eyes followed Sestianus as he quietly moved across the dungeon, bringing encouragement and comfort to all. All at once Quintus felt he was strongly tied to all these people who all believed in the same God, and who were awaiting the same fate. He recalled the days he had spent camping at the Campagna among the homeless. There too, they had been strongly united by the same plight, and yet everyone was left to himself. Even among those thousands of people one could feel very lonely. Here in this dungeon it was different. A superhuman spirit joined the people together.

Meanwhile the sun had risen higher. Beams of light shone through the barred openings that looked out upon the arena. The theatre slowly filled, and the shouting of the crowd could be heard clearly. This private arena of Nero was relatively small. Up to twenty-five thousand people could be seated here. All these people had come to see the Christians die. They yelled and whistled impatiently because Nero and his retinue had not yet arrived even though the official starting time had passed. The Emperor and his court were still too tired from the wild night of feasting in the palace gardens.

The guards, too, became impatient. If they ran behind schedule, they could never kill all the Christians waiting in the dungeons. It was already a very tight programme, even without the delay.

Naturally, the wild animals became even more restless because of the general commotion. They roared and whimpered heartrendingly, sticking their irritated noses through the bars to sniff the scent of the people and the food they carried with them.

Yet, all the noise could not disturb the peace and quiet in the dungeon. God Himself was present there.

Quintus looked at Caecillia. She was not leaning against Demas anymore, as she had done half an hour ago, but was sitting upright. Her face shone and it seemed as if she was not aware of what was happening around her. Quintus nudged his friend and beckoned to him to look at Caecillia. Demas nodded.

"I think her soul is already in heaven," he whispered. Unintentionally, they moved up a little out of the way. They were aware of something sacred next to them.

Quintus cautiously looked about him and discovered that more people were in a similar state, even some small children. Quintus felt wondrously light inside. He did not know that his face, too, began to shine. To die a martyr seemed unimportant to him now.

Outside the public shouted.

Suddenly the grille door opened and some soldiers entered the dungeon. With great care some men and women were selected and dragged outside roughly. Silently, the people that were left behind followed them with their eyes. Sestianus made the sign of a cross in the air and after that lifted up his hands to bless them.

"The grace of God and the love of Christ be with you," he said in a loud voice. This was "rewarded" with a whip-lash in his face but he did not appear to feel it. He knelt down and prayed for the first victims.

Loud shouting was heard from the arena.

"Hail to Caesar! Hail to Caesar!"

The Emperor had arrived at his Imperial Box. Trumpet-signals announced the start of the "games." It became quiet in the theatre. In a loud voice Tigellinus read out the programme.

"Our divine Caesar, son of the gods, is pleased to open the games in which the Christians will perform. During the morning-hours scenes from the Greek and Roman mythology will be enacted in a very realistic manner. For instance: 'Hercules at the stake;' 'Pasiphae fighting with the raging buffalo;' 'Orpheus devoured by the bear;' 'Laurelous at the cross,' etcetera, etcetera."

Loud cheering arose from the crowd as they settled themselves comfortably. They were in for a great spectacle. Their eyes, gleaming from alcohol and also the malaria plague in the city, were fixed upon the arena. The lions and tigers, the wolves, and wild dogs acted more violently now that they scented the first drops of blood.

"We'll just dress up the players for the next performance." The arena-servants grinned as they entered the dungeon. They grabbed several men, women, and children at random, and shamelessly tore off their clothing. Quickly and roughly the victims were sewn into fresh animal-skins. Tigellinus came down to have a look at the result of the "disguise." He nodded approvingly when he saw the people dressed in horse, reindeer, sheep, and other animals' skins.

"Now the wild dogs will surely have an appetite for them," he grinned. He lifted up a baby wrapped up in lamb's skin, to have a better look at it. The little child cried in protest.

Tigellinus was visibly nervous. The morning-programme had not offered what Nero and he had thought it would. Those self-conceited Christians simply refused to co-operate. Instead of killing or disgracing each other as was expected of them in the play, they knelt down to pray. Even the most severe threats and whip-lashes did not change their minds. Moreover, Nero was not pleased because the Christians did not give him the usual salutation. All gladiators, as they entered the arena, always placed themselves in front of Caesar, stretched out their right arm, and called, "Hail to Caesar; they who are going about to die salute you!"

No, the games with the Christians appeared to have degenerated into a grand failure. To put Nero and the public in a better mood, something different had to be done.

Then he saw Caecillia, still sitting in a corner of the dungeon.

"Take her along; she is a very beautiful girl," he ordered. Impulsively, Demas placed himself in front of the girl. The boy knew that Tigellinus had something special in mind. But he was roughly pushed aside.

"Goodbye, Caecillia. Till we meet again," Demas mumbled when the grille closed behind her. "May God be gracious to you." But then he became more vehement. "I must see what they are going to do to her!" Ignoring of the protests of Quintus and Sestianus, he pulled himself up at the bars of the gate to look into the arena.

There the remains of the mythological plays were being hastily cleaned up. Patches soaked with blood, were sprinkled with clean sand.

Then Caecillia entered the arena. Demas screamed with fright. The girl was naked! But, oblivious of the thousands of eyes looking at her, she walked to the middle of the arena and knelt down to pray. Her long, loose hair fell protectively about her body as a coat. Only her uplifted face could be seen clearly. The glorious light still radiated from her, giving her a sacred appearance. Even the public was influenced by it. Like Demas they looked on in fascination. The girl continued to pray. A trumpet signalled a bolt to be unfastened and a huge, ravenous Libyan lion was released. The animal blinked. The bright sunlight hurt its eyes. Dazed, he lay motionless. He scented prey. Slowly he turned his mighty head. There, in the middle of the arena he saw something edible. Slowly he stood up. With his head down, he roared fiercely. His strong teeth flashed in the sunlight. He stalked up to the girl while his tail swished the sand. Again he roared.

It seemed as if Caecillia did not notice the animal. She kept praying. All the spectators held their breath. Even Nero's interest was aroused. The lion came closer and closer, eyes fixed on his prey. Was he ready to pounce? . . . No, he was not! He lay down again and became silent. He only watched. Then the beast slid on his belly toward the girl, almost in submission. To everyone's great surprise the monster carefully put his enormous head into Caecillia's lap. She smiled as she stroked his mane.

"That lion doesn't even harm her," Demas stammered.

The emotion in the arena was intense. The lion was spellbound by Caecillia's sacredness!

From the Imperial Box everyone looked on in amazement. This had never happened before.

"Her God is protecting her," Seneca said softly. Startled Nero looked at him.

"Her God? Do the Christians have a real God?"

Seneca nodded without turning his eyes away from Caecillia and the lion. "They say that their God is the mightiest. He has created heaven and earth, and He rules man and animal, as you can see now. The Christians also claim that He determines life and death."

Fear came into Nero's eyes when he heard this. His breath failed him and a cold sweat rose on his brow. Nero was a coward. He was terribly afraid, of gods in particular, even though he alleged that he himself was a son of them.

"Does their God have the power over life and death?" he gasped. "Then He can kill me too, and that shouldn't happen!"

Suddenly that insane look came into his eyes again. He laughed hysterically. "Only I . . . I only . . . and nobody else can decide about life and death!" he screamed as he jumped up. "Who killed his own mother? I did! Who killed his own wife? I did! Who killed his brother? I did! Yes, whom did I not kill? Ten . . . no, twenty, hundreds, thousands I have killed. And who saved them when I decided to kill them? Nobody. Only I have the power over life and death."

His loud voice and mad laugh sounded over the arena. "Cut off her head!" he ordered. "I would like to see which God can save her from my sword. And then everybody will know that it is I who decide about life and death!"

Exhausted and profusely perspiring, Nero fell back in his marble seat. He looked on with interest as some slaves, armed with sharply pointed sticks, drove the lion back into its den. Caecillia was still on her knees, praying. It seemed as if she did not notice anything of what was happening around her.

Neither did she see the soldier who approached her with a drawn sword.

The soldier hesitated when he was close to the girl. As rough and callous as he was, he still fell under the spell of Caecillia. But then he regained composure. He did not have any choice but to obey the order. If he refused he himself would be punished with death. The girl would be decapitated anyway; if not by him then by another soldier.

A moment later Caecillia died.

A faint smile played about Nero's lips.

Resentful whispering was heard throughout the arena.

In the dungeon Demas sank to the floor, totally shocked. His face was ashen-gray.

"They beheaded her," he cried with horror. "I saw it!"

The boy cried and covered his face with his hands.

"I saw it! I saw it!" he continued to repeat.

Sestianus went to Demas.

"Caecillia is now with the Lord, and you should be thankful that she had died without suffering pain. She has felt nothing of it."

Demas jumped up.

"I must be thankful, you say?" he shouted. "That lion didn't touch her and yet she had to die. What is this God that we have?" he suddenly added with a hoarse cry. "A God who lets His followers be murdered!"

"You are mistaken," Sestianus said. "We have a God who takes His children home."

Demas laughed wretchedly.

"I hate God!" he then called out.

Immediately a guard dashed forward.

"Aha, is someone coming to their senses?" he asked through the bars. "Are you perhaps intending to sacrifice to the Emperor?"

"Sacrifice to the emperor, the murderer of my girlfriend? Never! Give me a sword, and I'll hack Nero into pieces!"

A centurion who heard the noise came up to Demas.

"By Mars, what do I hear? Is there a Christian here who wants to kill?" he asked sarcastically. With interest he looked at Demas. "Mmm, that lad has a good figure for the arena. Bring him to the School for Gladiators. Then soon he will have the opportunity to kill to his heart's content."

The gate was opened and Demas was seized. Two soldiers marched him off. Gradually, the shouting of the shocked and frustrated boy died down. In the dungeon the people were disheartened; the sacred atmosphere was spoiled.

"How good God is," Sestianus suddenly said. "He still gives Demas the opportunity to repent from his sin. He doesn't have to die today. Do you see that God understands people? He knows our weaknesses and He knows quite well that Demas was confused by the death of Caecillia. Let us pray that God will not allow him to harden his heart but that he will use the delay to repent."

"Will God be so merciful and forgive him even this sin?" somebody asked.

Sestianus nodded convincingly.

"Even Peter who denied his Saviour three times and afterward repented with a contrite heart had been granted forgiveness. And here, in this dungeon, we still have the task to pray for Demas because we are the only ones who are aware of his sin."

After these words the presbyter knelt down in the filthy straw, setting an example that was followed by all the others.

Nothing happened in the dungeon for some time, and so it appeared that the death of Caecillia had been the last item on the morning-programme. Through the barred windows the shouts from the amphitheatre and the bustle of thousands of voices was heard.

The starved animals, however, became more violent. For some hours they had scented blood and now were totally wild. Tigellinus listened to them with pleasure. This afternoon's spectacle would not be a failure, he thought. He was only concerned about the many Christians that were still in the dungeons. It was quite late already and there would not be time to clean the arena between the different events. But he did not let that worry him. Putting all else out of his head, Tigellinus went to lunch with Nero and his retinue.

But the prisoners were not aware of this. They were in good spirits again as the episode with Demas had gradually fallen into the background.

The Christians who had been sewn into animal skins were seated together praying. They understood very well that in a short while they would be the first to be thrown into the arena.

Slowly the sacred atmosphere of the morning returned. Quintus now experienced the same feeling as he had seen in the Christians at the torture-poles in Nero's gardens: a total surrender to God's will and the readiness to die an abominable death. He felt lighthearted and happy. Earthly things did not matter anymore.

Sestianus was still very busy encouraging and comforting the believers. Not everyone could free himself from this world without a struggle. The presbyter dearly wanted to celebrate the Holy Supper again with the prisoners. He asked the guard for bread and wine. To his disappointment it was refused. "It is not our custom to still feed those who will be fed to the wild animals," was the reply.

Sestianus looked the soldier straight into his eyes. "So we are food for the wild animals," he said softly. "Perhaps you are right." Then he folded his hands, looked upward and said in a loud voice which drowned the roaring of the lions, "I am the bread of God and the teeth of animals will grind me, so that I may be proved to be the real bread of Christ."

"Amen," they all answered.

The soldier shrugged his shoulders. He did not understand the Christians.

Outside a trumpet-signal sounded. The afternoon games were to commence. The soldiers became active. Slaves bent over the capstans to turn the lever that would open the prison-bars.

"Come on, you there in those skins. You have to perform!" one of the soldiers called out. The people scrambled to their feet while they were vigorously lashed. Sestianus again lifted up his hands over them.

"May the Lord bless you. May He make His face to shine upon you and be gracious to you. Amen."

With heads uplifted the Christians walked through the passage and out into the arena. When the public saw the people sewn into animal skins, they broke out in enthusiastic cheering. This could be great fun! The cheering died down when the condemned men and women started to sing a Psalm: "The LORD is my Shepherd . . ."

Then they knelt down to pray. Neither the whip-lashes nor the snarled orders to salute the Emperor had any effect. At his wit's end, Tigellinus commanded the cages of the wild dogs to be opened.

The pack came tearing out, yelping and growling. The scent of fresh animal skins had stimulated them. The leader of the pack ripped at a man's throat. The dogs howled. The first drops of blood had been tasted and the starved beasts became mad with thirst for more blood. Soon nobody could tell what was happening. Wild twisting and turning of bodies and skins was all that could be seen. In the middle of the fray two dogs were fighting over the body of a woman.

When the dogs had satisfied their initial passion, the public became bored and the shout was heard, "Now the lions, Caesar!"

Nero signalled and a new group of Christians were driven into the arena: men, women, and children. Amid the remains of those who had already been torn to pieces, they knelt down and prayed. Suddenly one of them — a woman — started to sing. Others joined in, and while the lions were ready to pounce upon them, an impressive choir sang,

*Exalt with us Christ's name,*
*Who helped us in our strife;*
*He gave us by His death*
*Blessed, everlasting life!*

Then the lions and tigers fell upon them and the singing was extinguished. Only the roaring of the wild beasts filled the air. The audience shouted and stretched their necks in order not to miss anything of the spectacle. It seemed as if all hell had broken loose. The animals ran to and fro, carrying parts of bodies in their mouths or looking for more prey. Slowly the blood coloured the arena's floor red, and the hot August sun soon made the smell nauseating.

After some time the lions and tigers had eaten their fill, and with swollen bellies they dragged themselves back to their cages. Some of them vomited, and others slipped on the remains of God's children.

Then it was the turn of the group to which Quintus and Sestianus belonged.

"Brothers and sisters," the presbyter said, "Now the moment has arrived in which it has pleased God to call us up. Do not fear! Only a short-lived suffering is awaiting you, and after that you will enter into the joy of God's glory. Therefore, lift up your hearts to God and entrust yourselves to Him in peace."

After this blessing, Sestianus left the dungeon at the head of the group. The others followed, joyous and full of trust. It was not necessary that the soldiers lashed them. But why then did they do it? Perhaps they were afraid of the Christians, and of their God!

Quintus walked as if in a dream. It seemed to him that he was approaching a wonderful shining light. Unconsciously he started to sing,

*Come let us then praise Christ, our Lord,*
*Who frees us from death; may he be adored.*
*With joyous heart now look up high,*
*e'en when the end of life is nigh.*

*When our mortal bodies turn to dust,*
*Christ comes to claim our soul, we trust.*
*Then we will sing our praise to God,*
*in heavenly places He will allot.*

The others immediately joined in and so a mighty choir entered the arena. The many mutilated corpses offered a gruesome welcome. But the Christians did not notice. Their souls were already on their way to heaven. They did not see that their feet became red with the blood that lay in large puddles on the ground. Occasionally one of the group needed support when he was in danger of tripping over or slipping on a partly-eaten body. With radiant faces they walked on. Sestianus went to where Nero was seated and stopped directly in front of him. The Emperor, seated on his marble chair, sat upright. Was, at last, one of the Christian dogs going to bring him, Nero, the required salute?

Sestianus pointed his finger toward Caesar. In a clear voice that could be heard throughout the amphitheatre he said, "Woe to you, Child of Satan! One day our blood will be claimed from your hand. Tremble, and don't forget that God shall demand an explanation of what you have done with the power with which He has clothed you."

Amused, Nero lent forward.

"Who is able or is so daring as to call me, mighty Caesar, son of the gods, to account?" he asked scornfully.

"God!"

"Who is that God who thinks he is mightier than I am? I rule over the whole known and civilised world, don't I?"

"But it is only by God's permission that you sit on the throne. He also rules over another world, unknown to you, which is called 'heaven.' You can still repent to that God. It is not too late."

Nero fell back in his seat, laughing.

Sestianus turned away and joined the others.

Amid mutilated bodies the Christians knelt down. Already before the lions attacked them, they were stained with the blood of the previous martyrs but they did not notice it. Neither did they hear the shouting which rose from thousands of throats when the wild animals were released from their cages. Quintus even smiled at the tiger that crept toward him. The last thing he saw was the animal baring his teeth and pounce on him. After that he lost consciousness.

Nero had become restless because of the admonishing words spoken by Sestianus, and he now completely lost his senses. With ever shortening intervals he ordered more Christians and more wild beasts into the arena. His mind needed distraction.

The arena was now a horrible spectacle. The bodies of the Christians totally covered the ground. At some places they were even lying on top of each other. The blood gave the white marble around the arena a reddish tinge.

The wild mass of animals were beyond recognition, as they heaved through the bodies. Raging bulls, crushing everything under their hooves, fought with lions and tigers. Bears and jackals growled as they ran to and fro. Christians were still standing in some places. It was a writhing mass of men and beasts, painted in one colour only: red!

The spectators were ecstatic because of this devilish scene. The people screamed above the roaring and bellowing of the beasts of prey. Some women went into hysterics and others fainted. A few lost their senses so much that they jumped over the balustrade into the arena, where they were immediately trampled upon and devoured.

Nero's face was as white as chalk. He tightened his thin lips; his eyes were wide-open. He had called for the powers of darkness and they had supreme rule over the arena.

"Do you think they don't like the performance?" he asked, pointing to some spectators who could no longer bear to look at the revolting scene and were leaving the amphitheatre.

Nobody answered. Even for the most hardened Roman this spectacle was too much. The only ones who were impressed by this hell, were the Christians who were still being driven into the arena. These believers saw God the Father who sent His angels to fetch the souls of the martyrs.

The public became impressed by the Christians' attitude. Was their God so powerful that His followers could walk into that loathsome arena without hesitation?

Many more people left, and long before closing-time the theatre was empty. The rage of the beasts of prey declined too. They were more than satiated, and exhausted from the unexpected fights. Many animals had also been killed! They dragged themselves back to their cages, their hair stiff with blood.

The devil withdrew too. With satisfaction he looked at where he had been allowed to reign for only a few hours. Yet, he had not been victorious. Christ had remained triumphant. Thanks be to God!

# CHAPTER 12

## *THE TASK*

When Quintus regained conciousness, he was immediately aware of a stinging pain in his shoulder. Confused, he tried to sit up but he soon found that this was impossible. Something was on top of him. As he remained on his back, he tried to put his mind straight. Where was he? He had died, had he not? Then he must be in heaven. But why then was it so very dark around him? And what about that pain in his shoulder? In heaven there was no darkness and there would not be any pain either. Slowly it dawned on Quintus that he was still alive. By a great wonder his life had been saved! A prayer of thanksgiving welled up in his heart. Yet he had to get used to the idea that he was still in the land of the living. "What intention could God have?" he asked himself.

For a long time Quintus brooded over this question while the pain in his shoulder made him lose consciousness periodically. Carefully he felt his shoulder. It appeared that a tiger had bitten him but the animal must have been distracted and had not worried about its prey any longer.

Quintus considered that more people had possibly survived. They had been taken out of the arena, severely injured, of course, but still alive.

Nobody checked if every victim was really dead. Unmoved by the scene, the arena-slaves shovelled the remains of men and animals into carts, which were then driven out of the arena heavily laden. Behind the arena, the remains were gathered into a large pit, and afterward the pit would be set on fire. Later it was to be filled in.

Having accertained that he was lying in the pit, Quintus tried to get out. This required a lot of effort because the body of a dead lion was lying across him. The loss of blood had also weakened him considerably. With extreme will-power, he succeeded in pulling himself up and climbed out of the pit.

Once on firm ground, he took a minute to get back to his senses. The pain in his shoulder was almost unbearable. He must have lost consciousness again for suddenly he saw torch-light close by. On hands and feet he crept away. Sheltered by a bush, he looked on as the slaves silently performed their lugubrious duty. He shuddered. After about ten minutes the road was clear again. "Where should he go?" he asked himself. He decided to try to reach Aquila's house, and he hoped that the Jew had not been arrested.

Limping heavily, Quintus started on his way. He had hardly covered a hundred metres when the mass grave was set alight. Again he had just escaped death.

"If you still have a task in this world, God will surely make your flight successful." Who had said that to him? Oh yes, it was Sestianus, at the time they had been taken prisoners. Well, he had not been given a chance to flee. So why had God now saved him in such a miraculous way? This question stuck in his mind. Therefore, he still had a task. But what was it? Perhaps Aquila could help him to figure this out. Supporting himself against a wall, Quintus dragged himself along. Every now and then he was overcome with giddiness, and he felt terribly weak and miserable. His shoulder bothered him more and more. Yet he stumbled on. How and where he walked he did not know. When, at last, he found himself at the tent factory on the Aventine hill, he could not explain how he had managed to get there. He could not remember one moment of the agonising walk through Rome's streets.

Aquila and Priscilla could not tell what had happened either, because the next day, very early in the morning, they found him lying on the steps of the house. They thought at first that he was dead but the doctor of Pudens was hastily called and he assured them that Quintus was only unconscious.

"A severe loss of blood has made him very weak."

"Poor boy," Priscilla said softly while watching the physician treating the patient. She skillfully came to the doctors aid when called upon.

"Do you know how he received these terrible injuries?"

"No. This morning we found him lying on our steps. We have not seen him since the morning before the fire."

"I ask this because the shoulder-injury was probably caused by a wild animal," the doctor explained.

Priscilla turned pale.

"Then I'm sure he has been in the arena," she said.

"But nobody can escape alive from there," Aquila joined in the conversation. "The stories I've heard about that place . . ."

"But where else could a tiger or lion have struck him?" the physician asked.

Nobody could answer that question.

"I sincerely hope you are right," Priscilla said suddenly.

The Jew and the doctor looked at the woman in amazement.

"Yes, I mean what I'm saying. It would suggest that Quintus had become a Christian, too."

Now the two men understood what the woman meant.

"If you are right, we can thank God for His two-fold blessing," Aquila answered.

The doctor nodded. Priscilla said, "I wish I could ask the boy."

"You must have patience, Priscilla. The boy is very weak and has a very high wound-fever. I can't even say for certain that he will survive," the physician said. "Let us pray to God and ask Him for recovery."

They left the room where Quintus was lying and called together all the workers of the tent factory. In a few words Aquila told them what had happened. The people were shocked when they heard the news. They knew Quintus so well. They were happy with the return of Quintus until somebody wondered where Demas and Caecillia could be. The atmosphere again became sober. So many of their acquaintances had disappeared without a trace lately.

"Maybe Quintus had still seen them," somebody suggested.

"If that is true, I'm afraid they will have died in the arena," Aquila sighed.

The following days were spent in suspense. Quintus was very ill. He had a very high temperature and was delirious for much of the time. Sometimes he mentioned the names of Demas, Caecillia, and Sestianus but most of the time he was unintelligible. Every now and then he opened his eyes but he did not recognise anybody. Day and night, Aquila and Priscilla took turns to be at the boy's sick-bed. During the daily gatherings in the atrium, prayer meetings were held to remember, not only the persecuted brothers and sisters but also Quintus.

And so the days went by. After a week the physician announced with joy that the critical stage was over.

"But grant the boy ample time for recovery," he warned. "Don't force him to speak just to satisfy your curiosity. He is still extremely weak. If he pulls through completely, it will be only thanks to God's grace."

It took another two weeks before Quintus could answer the questions asked by Aquila and his wife. In a weak voice, and sometimes without any logical connection, he related what had happened to him since he had been sent on an errand to Hermes' house.

Tears welled in Priscilla's eyes when he told them about the death of his mother.

"May I, in the future, take your mother's place?" she asked.

Quintus nodded and his pale eyes shone.

Then he told them about his baptism and his first celebration of the Lord's Supper.

"Lord, how good Thou art!" Aquila said.

He and his wife were very moved when he told them what happened to Caecillia and Demas. Then suddenly he stopped. He had nothing else to say.

"Can't you remember anything of what has happened to you in the arena?"

"No, nothing. When I try to remember, it is as if I'm looking into a dazzling light."

"You can be thankful for that," Aquila reckoned, "otherwise the memory of it might haunt you for the rest of your life."

Priscilla beckoned to her husband that it was time to leave the sick boy alone.

"The boy — our boy — needs rest, Aquila."

The news about the death of Caecillia brought great dejection in Aquila's and Pudens' house.

"I wished the children had stayed home," Claudia sighted, "then nothing would have happened to them. Here at home it is still safe, because Nero is careful not to harm Christians who have respect in the community. But Caecillia and Demas so dearly wanted to go to the meeting in the catacombs that I, at last, gave them my permission. I thought, 'Surely, God will protect them.' "

"Yet all these terrible events have been turned into good, Claudia," Pudens answered. "Now they've met Quintus when he needed their support most. More importantly for Demas, he still has a chance to save his life, while Caecillia has, by her death, glorified God's name. Isn't that the greatest task a human being can be given?"

"Yes, I agree with you, but it's all so terribly difficult to accept," the woman sighed.

The next day Quintus presented Aquila with a big problem. He told the Jew that he saw his wonderful rescue as a sign from God.

"And now that I'm recovering from a very serious illness, what task does God really have in mind for me, Aquila?" he concluded.

The Jew was quiet for a long time, thinking deeply before he said, "Perhaps I know. Demas' life was saved after his terrible sin; he still has time to repent. In the dungeon all the Christians present remembered him in their prayer to God. Now that they have all died none of them could make intercession for Demas anymore. Outside the arena nobody knows what has befallen him. You are the only one who knows, Quintus. You have been saved and told us about Demas. Now you have the opportunity to try and bring the boy back to God. You can also urge us to pray for him. This could be your task but possibly, your task is even greater. Perhaps you have to go into the world to witness of Christ and of your miraculous deliverance."

Quintus needed time to think this over; it was all very vague and unreal.

"But why does God make everything so complicated?" he asked. "Why was it necessary to burn Rome to promote His kingdom and in that way place it in the centre of the people's attention? Why must all those Christians suffer so terribly to bring others to repentance? Why did Demas have to curse God and why was I spared? To bring him back to God? Why? It can be done much simpler, can it not? I don't understand God."

"I can't understand Him either," Aquila answered. "And that is fortunate."

"Fortunate? But I want to understand God."

The Jew shook his head.

"Quintus, if you with your imperfect human understanding, could comprehend God, what a powerless being God would be. Then He wouldn't be greater than we are. No, Quintus, be glad you cannot understand God and be thankful when He occasionally lifts up a tip of the veil to indicate what

His intentions are. Just believe this: despite everything, God is and remains full of love, righteousness, and grace. Surely, God is good!"

Quintus smiled and stretched himself on his bed.

Aquila retreated and the boy was left by himself.

In the garden a bird was singing.

Quintus listened to it until he fell asleep. His last thought was: "I have a task, and God is good!"

# Brief biographies of the historical people who appear in this story

## Nero

Nero was the son of Agrippina. She was particularly power-hungry and nothing could stop her to achieve her aim. She had a brazen character and executed her will shamelessly.

In an evil manner she managed to become the wife of Emperor Claudius, with the intention to make Nero his successor. Agrippina poisoned Emperor Claudius, and Nero became emperor of the Roman Empire.

After Nero came to power, Agrippina noticed that her influence over him began to lessen. This irritated her. She had anticipated that when Nero was emperor, she too would improve her position. Her whole plan threatened to fall to pieces. Agrippina then tried to gain power in another way. Emperor Claudius had another son and to get him onto the throne appeared the only option. For her plan to be successful, her son Nero needed to be killed, but this did not bother her. Nero discovered the plot, and had his brother murdered. He followed this up later by killing his mother as well.

He also had his wife Octavia murdered because he was scared that she too was plotting against him.

## Aquila and Priscilla

Aquila was Jewish, and worked as tent-maker in Rome. Here he met Priscilla and married her.

In A.D. 52 all Jews were temporarily banished from Rome. Aquila and his wife left to stay in Corinth, where they met the apostle Paul (Acts 18:1-4). Paul and Aquila became friends. There is more than enough evidence to presume that Aquila and Priscilla, after their return to Rome, did much of the groundwork in the establishing of the first Christian congregation. Their names are often mentioned in the letters of Paul. Priscilla is sometimes called Prisca. This is a normal shortening of her name.

## Caecillia

The events in the arena are based on fact, although some of these took place in later periods of persecution.

# Other Great Books from Inheritance Publications

**BIBLE STORIES For Our Little Ones**
**by W.G. VAN DE HULST**
**Illustrated by J.H. Isings**

This book is intended to be a book for mothers. A book to be read in quiet hours, to little ones of four to seven or eight years old who sit at Mother's knee. A book to be read slowly, yes, especially slowly; very clearly with warm, loving reverence and awe which creates in little children's heart a pious reverence and a joy filled awe. It desires to be a BIBLE FOR THE LITTLE ONES, reaching out to all areas of a child's understanding. A child does not comprehend everything, yet understands a great deal. This story bible wishes to tell about the holy things in plain, clear, almost simple language, which still must never profane the consecrated happenings. It is not meant to be complete. Completeness would hinder children.

This book is not meant to be anything but a modest, reverent endeavour to lead the little ones into the holy sphere of Godly things. The interest of the little ones will be the test to see whether this endeavour is accomplished. May God give our little ones His wonderful blessings in the quiet hours, listening to His voice at Mother's knee.
— The Author

**Subject: Bible**
**ISBN 1-894666-69-0**

**Age: 7-10**
**Can.$29.95 U.S.$24.90**

## The Heroes of Castle Bretten
## by Margaret S. Comrie

Eleonore, Lady of Castle Bretten, has been alienated from her friends and allies by false rumours spread by her nephew, General Lucas von Ruprecht, Count of Zamosc. When Guido, a young Protestant, comes to live at the castle, he wins the love and trust of Lady Eleonore and Felix, the General's son. With lots of excitement and action Guido and Felix uncover a plot to gain control of the castle.

**Time: 1618-1648**
**ISBN 1-894666-65-8**

**Age: 11-99**
**Can.$14.95 U.S.$12.90**

## Augustine, The Farmer's Boy of Tagaste
## by P. De Zeeuw

C. MacDonald in *The Banner of Truth*: Augustine was one of the great teachers of the Christian Church, defending it against many heretics. This interesting publication should stimulate and motivate all readers to extend their knowledge of Augustine and his works.
J. Sawyer in *Trowel & Sword*: . . . It is informative, accurate historically and theologically, and very readable. My daughter loved it (and I enjoyed it myself). An excellent choice for home and church libraries.

**Time: A.D. 354-430**
**ISBN 0-921100-05-1**

**Age: 9-99**
**Can.$7.95 U.S.$6.90**

### William III and the Revolution of 1688
### and *Gustavus Adolphus II*
## 2 Historical Essays by Marjorie Bowen

F.G. Oosterhoff in *Reformed Perspective*: I recommend this book without any hesitation. The two biographies make excellent reading, and the times the essays describe are of considerable interest and importance in the history of our civilization. Moreover, although Bowen obviously is not one in faith with Gustavus Adolphus and William of Orange, her essays relate incidents that are testimonials to God's mercies in preserving His Church. Remembering these mercies, we may take courage for the present and for the future.

Time: 1630-1689                                   **Age: 14-99**
ISBN 0-921100-06-X                      **Can.\$9.95 U.S.\$7.95**

# The Huguenot Inheritance Series

### *The Escape* by A. Van der Jagt
### The Adventures of Three Huguenot Children
### Fleeing Persecution
### Huguenot Inheritance Series #1

F. Pronk in *The Messenger*: This book . . . will hold its readers spellbound from beginning to end. The setting is late seventeenth century France. Early in the story the mother dies and the father is banished to be a galley slave for life on a war ship. Yet in spite of threats and punishment, sixteen-year-old John and his ten-year-old sister Manette, refuse to give up the faith they have been taught.

Time: 1685-1695                                 **Age: 12-99**
ISBN 0-921100-04-3                     **Can.\$11.95 U.S.\$9.95**

### *The Secret Mission*
### by A. Van der Jagt
### A Huguenot's Dangerous Adventures
### in the Land of Persecution
### Huguenot Inheritance Series #2

In the sequel to our best-seller, *The Escape,* John returns to France with a secret mission of the Dutch Government. At the same time he attempts to find his father.

Time: 1702-1712                         **Age: 12-99**
ISBN 0-921100-18-3               **Can.\$14.95 U.S.\$12.95**

### *How They Kept The Faith*
### by Grace Raymond
### A Tale of the Huguenots
### of Languedoc
### Huguenot Inheritance Series #3

Christine Farenhorst in *Christian Renewal*: Presenting a moving account of the weals and woes of two Huguenot families during the heavy waves of persecution in seventeenth century France, this book, although its onset is a bit slow, is fascinating and moving reading. Covering all aspects of Huguenot life during this difficult time period, this goodsized paperback volume is a well-spring of encouragement for Christians today and highly recommended as reading for all those age twelve and over.

Time: 1676-1686                               **Age: 13-99**
ISBN 0-921100-64-7               **Can.\$14.95 U.S.\$12.90**

### The Young Huguenots by Edith S. Floyer
### Huguenot Inheritance Series #4

It was a happy life at the pretty chateau. Even after that dreadful Sunday evening, when strange men came down and shut the people out of the church, not much changed for the four children. Until the soldiers came . . .

**Time: 1686-1687**

**ISBN 0-921100-65-5**

**Age: 11-99**

**Can.$11.95 U.S.$9.90**

### Driven into Exile
### by Charlotte Maria Tucker
### A Story of the Huguenots
### Huguenot Inheritance
### Series #5

Christine Farenhorst in *Christian Renewal*: "Set in the days following the Revocation of the Edict of Nantes, (an edict in effect from 1598-1685 providing religious freedom for the French Protestants), this story follows the lives of two Huguenot families. Losing all to remain constant, the La Force family flees to Britain, while the Duval family remains in France. Suspenseful, the unfolding panorama of persecution and intrigue is well-suited for twenty-first century church goers who take freedom of religion for granted."

**Time: 1685-1695**

**ISBN 0-921100-66-3**

**Age: 13-99**

**Can.$9.95 U.S.$8.90**

### The Refugees by A. Conan Doyle
### A Tale of Two Continents
### Huguenot Inheritance Series #6

*The Refugees* is a fast-paced exciting historical novel filled with daring and adventure. It depicts the escape of Louis De Catinat and his cousin from France after the revocation of the Edict of Nantes in 1685. Fleeing aboard a merchant vessel they attempt to reach America but find themselves stranded on an iceberg. The result is a hazardous trek through Canadian forests, avoiding both Roman Catholic Frenchmen and savage Indians.

Follow the adventures of well to do people, bereft of all convenience and fleeing for their lives to seek refuge in a country where freedom of religion returns stability to their lives.

**Time: 1685-1686**

**ISBN 0-921100-67-1**

**Age: 12-99**

**Can.$17.95 U.S.$14.90**

### Done and Dared in Old France
### by Deborah Alcock
### Huguenot Inheritance Series #7

Christine Farenhorst wrote in *Christian Renewal*: Ten-year-old Gaspard, accidentally separated from his parents, is raised by a group of outlaw salt runners who fear neither God nor man. . . . Through the providence of God, Gaspard's heart turns to Him in faith and after a series of adventures is able to flee France to the safer Protestant shores of England. Fine and absorbing reading. Deborah Alcock has wonderful vocabulary, is a marvelous story-teller, and brings out the amazing hand of God's almighty power in every chapter. Highly recommended.

**Time: 1685-1697**

**ISBN 1-894666-03-8**

**Age: 11-99**

**Can.$14.95 U.S.$12.90**

### *It Began With a Parachute* by **William R. Rang**

Fay S. Lapka in *Christian Week*: [It] . . . is a well-told tale set in Holland near the end of the Second World War. . . The story, although chock-full of details about life in war-inflicted Holland, remains uncluttered, warm, and compelling.

**Time: 1940-1945**                         **Age: 9-99**
**ISBN 0-921100-38-8**             **Can.$8.95 U.S.$7.90**

### *No More Singing* by **Norman Bomer**
### *with colour illustrations by G. Carol Bomer*

No More Singing is a poignant allegory, beautifully told, that will move many children to an understanding that the aborting of our children is legal [according to the governing authorities].

As parents read this story to their children and explain the sad truth of abortion, conviction will

grow in young hearts. As that conviction is strengthened and nurtured, it will draw us nearer to that day when protection is again restored to all children.

    — Curtis J. Young

**Subject: Pro life**                       **Age: 10-99**
**ISBN 0-88815-566-2**         **Can.$5.95 U.S.$4.90**

# Struggle for Freedom Series by Piet Prins

David Engelsma in the *Standard Bearer*: This is reading for Reformed children, young people, and (if I am any indication) their parents. It is the story of 12-year-old Martin Meulenberg and his family during the Roman Catholic persecution of the Reformed Christians in The Netherlands about the year 1600. A peddlar, secretly distributing Reformed books from village to village, drops a copy of Guido de Brès' *True Christian Confession* — a booklet forbidden by the Roman Catholic authorities. An evil neighbor sees the book and informs . . .

**Time: 1568-1572**                            **Age: 10-99**

**Vol. 1 -** *When The Morning Came*
      **ISBN 0-921100-12-4**       **Can.$11.95 U.S.$9.90**
**Vol. 2 -** *Dispelling the Tyranny*
      **ISBN 0-921100-40-X**      **Can.$11.95 U.S.$9.90**
**Vol. 3 -** *The Beggars' Victory*
      **ISBN 0-921100-53-1**      **Can.$11.95 U.S.$9.90**

## *Salt in His Blood — The Life of Michael De Ruyter*
### by William R. Rang

Liz Buist in *Reformed Perspective*: This book is a fictional account of the life of Michael de Ruyter, who as a schoolboy already preferred life at sea to being at school. De Ruyter is known as the greatest Dutch admiral, who, in spite of his successful career as a sailor captain and pirate hunter, remained humble and faithful to his God who had called him to serve his country. The author brings to life many adventures at sea that keep the reader spellbound, eager to know what the next chapter will bring. . . This book is highly recommended as a novel way to acquiring knowledge of a segment of Dutch history, for avid young readers and adults alike.

**Time: 1607-1676**                    **Age: 10-99**
**ISBN 0-921100-59-0**          **Can.$10.95 U.S.$9.90**

## *The Shadow Series*
### by Piet Prins

One of the most exciting series of a master story teller about the German occupation of The Netherlands during the emotional time of the Second World War (1940-1945).

K. Bruning in *Una Sancta* about Vol.4 - The Partisans, and Vol. 5 - Sabotage: . . . the country was occupied by the German military forces. The nation's freedom was destroyed by the foreign men in power. Violence, persecutions and executions were the order of the day, and the main target of the enemy was the destruction of the christian way of life. In that time the resistance movement of underground fighters became very active. People from all ages and levels joined in and tried to defend the Dutch Christian heritage as much as possible. The above mentioned books show us how older and younger people were involved in that dangerous struggle. It often was a life and death battle. Every page of these books is full of tension. The stories give an accurate and very vivid impression of that difficult and painful time. These books should also be in the hands of our young people. They are excellent instruments to understand the history of their own country and to learn the practical value of their own confession and Reformed way of life. What about as presents on birthdays?

**Time: 1944-1945**                                                                        **Age: 10-99**

| | | |
|---|---|---|
| **Vol. 1  The Lonely Sentinel** | **ISBN 1-894666-72-0** | **Can.$9.95 U.S.$8.90** |
| **Vol. 2  Hideout in the Swamp** | **ISBN 1-894666-73-9** | **Can.$9.95 U.S.$8.90** |
| **Vol. 3  The Grim Reaper** | **ISBN 1-894666-74-7** | **Can.$9.95 U.S.$8.90** |
| **Vol. 4  The Partisans** | **ISBN 0-921100-07-8** | **Can.$9.95 U.S.$8.90** |
| **Vol. 5  Sabotage** | **ISBN 0-921100-08-6** | **Can.$9.95 U.S.$8.90** |

### Anak, the Eskimo Boy by Piet Prins

F. Pronk in *The Messenger*: Anak is an Eskimo Boy, who, with his family, lives with the rest of their tribe in the far north. The author describes their day-to-day life as they hunt for seals, caribou, and walruses. Anak is being prepared to take up his place as an adult and we learn how he is introduced to the tough way of life needed to survive in the harsh northern climate. We also learn how Anak and his father get into contact with the white man's civilization. . . This book makes fascinating reading, teaching about the ways of Eskimos, but also of the power of the Gospel. Anyone over eight years old will enjoy this book and learn from it.

**Subject: Eskimos / Mission**      **Age: 7-99**
**ISBN 0-921100-11-6**      **Can.$6.95 U.S.$6.30**

### Stefan Derksen's Polar Adventure by Piet Prins

*One of the sailors, who was known to be a good shot, decided to try to hit the bear while they were still in the boat. But because his footing was unsteady, he almost missed. The polar bear suffered only a light flesh wound . . . The sailor tried to shoot again, but the gun misfired. It seemed only seconds, and the angry animal had reached the boat. It laid its front paws on the edge and tried to climb in.*

Once again Piet Prins has given us an outstanding novel. Follow Stefan's adventure as he runs away from his cruel uncle the cobbler and joins the men aboard the whaling ship the *Sea Dragon*. Hunting whales, encountering ferocious polar bears, storms and fog, dealing with sickness and hunger, floating adrift and shipwreck, all become part of Stefan Derksen's polar adventure. It is an adventure full of distress and surprise. Will Stefan ever return home to his mother?

**Time: 1674-1675**      **Age: 9-99**
**ISBN 1-894666-67-4**      **Can.$11.95 U.S.$9.90**

### Scout: The Haunted Castle by Piet Prins

Tom and Scout are on vacation with Tom's two best friends, Carl and Bert, and his sisters, Ina and Miriam. On their rambles through the woods, the group of young people are stopped one day by customs officials. They are accused of being in league with a gang of criminals who are smuggling goods across the nearby German border. Scout's reputation as a tracking dog has preceded him, and soon the young people are helping both the police and the customs officials. The mystery of the haunted castle, a coded message hidden under a tree, a gang of smugglers that can vanish at will, a burglary without clues — they all come together when Tom and Scout tumble over a four-hundred-year-old secret. Suddenly, however, Tom is no longer looking for adventure but fighting for his very life.

**Subject: Fiction**      **Age: 9-99**
**ISBN 1-894666-44-5**      **Can.$9.95 U.S.$8.90**

### Scout: The Flying Phantom by Piet Prins

When Tom and his friends Bert and Carl set out on an adventure over spring vacation, they are only looking for a good time. But soon a series of baffling events draws them inexorably into another mystery. What connection is there between a dangerous poacher, a police cap on top of a tower, a host of unsolved burglaries, and a mysterious fire? Is the fearsome character who walks on the swamp the ghost of the legendary Flying Phantom? Or is it something or someone else?

Join the boys, Tom's dog, Scout, and their mutual friend Captain Brandenburg as they muster courage, tenacity, and wit to track a very unusual kind of criminal.

**Subject: Fiction**      **Age: 9-99**
**ISBN 1-894666-45-3**      **Can.$9.95 U.S.$8.90**

### Scout: The Sailing Sleuths by Piet Prins

While Tom and his two friends are making plans for a vacation, Carl's father announces that he has acquired a sailboat, as part of a business deal. The three boys see the chance for a very unusual holiday.

Their peaceful sailing trip is sabotaged when they run into a gang of notorious carnival followers who put on sidewalk shows as a cover for more profitable sidelines. After a confrontation with the gang, the three sailors and Scout find themselves in trouble with the police. Their attempt to clear themselves leads to a wild chase through rivers, canals, and lakes. When at last the boys come face to face with the gang and its ruthless leader, they are stranded on an island in the middle of an isolated lake. In the showdown they are all alone — except for Scout.

**Subject: Fiction**  **Age: 9-99**
**ISBN 1-894666-46-1**  **Can.$9.95 U.S.$8.90**

### Scout: The Treasure of Rodensteyn Castle by Piet Prins

When they are invited to spend a few weeks with Uncle Arnie at the seashore, little do Tom, Carl, and Bert realize that they will be staying in the hunting lodge of a medieval castle. Uncle Arnie is quite a storyteller. Soon the boys find their imaginations and the lodge peopled with ghosts from Rodensteyn Castle, a castle long ago buried under the sand. But do ghosts leave tracks, tracks that Scout follows into the sea? Are the legends of the ghost of Sir Isobald and the treasure of Rodensteyn Castle true? Is it a ghost that Tom spots in the dunes at night? Can Scout's nose, no matter how keen, help the boys solve a mystery over 400 years old? Past and present, fact and fiction merge as Tom and his friends search for a treasure that has outlasted the ages.

**Subject: Fiction**  **Age: 9-99**
**ISBN 1-894666-47-X**  **Can.$9.95 U.S.$8.90**

### Scout: The Mystery of the Abandoned Mill by Piet Prins

Tom, Carl, and Bert are spending the summer on the farm. One day they run into a large, surly man with a black monster of a dog. Scout and the black dog are enemies at first sight. The man arouses the boys' suspicions at once. He is no ordinary vacationer. When Scout pulls a boy from the river, the boys make a friend. From the boy's mother they hear a story about the abandoned mill and a missing treasure. The story draws them into an adventure that sets the boys on a collision course with the dangerous man and his equally dangerous dog. Trying to play the master detective, Tom leads his friends into a desperate situation. Can they stop Scout from clashing with the powerful black dog as he rushes to their aid? After all their hard work, will the boys lose the treasure after all? Worse yet, will the crook decide to kill the only witnesses to his crime?

**Subject: Fiction**  **Age: 9-99**
**ISBN 1-894666-48-8**  **Can.$9.95 U.S.$8.90**

### Scout's Distant Journey by Piet Prins

Scout's seventh adventure reacquaints us with his three friends and introduces some new characters. One is Uncle Bob, long absent in North America but now back in the old country where he and his wife settle into a small but honest-to-goodness castle! Naturally Tom and his friends, including Scout, are invited to spend the summer holidays at Uncle Bob's intriguing house. Actually, the invitation is more like a challenge: Uncle Bob pretends to have a low opinion of "modern youth;" he thinks they're soft and over-pampered. To prove him wrong, Tom and his friends decide to travel on foot. But on the journey, little goes right: disasters dog their footsteps and danger is their constant companion . . . Their arrival marks both victory and defeat . . .

**Subject: Fiction**  **Age: 9-99**
**ISBN 1-894666-49-6**  **Can.$9.95 U.S.$8.90**

### Martin Shows the Way by Cor Van Rijswijk
#### Series: In Father's Footsteps

It was cold and dark outside. Yet there were some boys walking in the streets.

They were going from one house to an other. Do you know what they were doing? Listen! They were singing. Suddenly a door was opened. A kind woman gave the boys something to eat. How happy they were.

**Time: 1483-1546**        **Age: 4-9**
**ISBN 1-894666-80-1**        **Can.$9.95 U.S.$8.90**

*The books in the* Series: In Father's Footsteps *are independent stories written by Cor Van Rijswijk about important people in Church History.*

*Read them to your four or five-year-old, and let your six or seven-year-old use them as readers.*

### John is Not Afraid by Cor Van Rijswijk
#### Series: In Father's Footsteps

John Knox was smart. He could study very well and learn quickly. Father and Mother really liked that. One day, John was called to go to his father. "John," he said, "you are a big boy now. You must either work, or keep going to school."

**Time: 1513?-1572**        **Age: 4-9**
**ISBN 1-894666-81-X**        **Can.$9.95 U.S.$8.90**

### William of Orange - The Silent Prince
#### by W.G. Van de Hulst

Whether you are old or young you will enjoy this biography on the life of William of Orange. Read it and give it as a birthday present to your children or grandchildren. A fascinating true story about one of the greatest princes who ever lived and already by his contemporaries justly compared to King David.

**Time: 1533-1584**        **Age: 7-99**
**ISBN 0-921100-15-9**        **Can.$11.95 U.S.$9.90**

### The Search for Sheltie
#### by Piet Prins

Having shaken the curse of Urumbu, Jack and Sheltie return to the old country. Injured in a traffic accident, Jack is laid up in a Genoa hospital. Sheltie goes on ahead to Rotterdam where he promptly gets lost.

This book gives a fascinating look at the "psychology" of a dog trying to avoid capture as he hunts doggedly for his master. It also tells the story of the extensive, persistent search Jack and his nephews make for Sheltie.

Unaccustomed to civilization, Sheltie faces danger at every turn. Several scrapes with death make this a real nail-biter!

**Subject: Fiction**        **Age: 9-99**
**ISBN 1-894666-43-7**        **Can.$9.95 U.S.$8.90**